SPACE PRECINCT

Based on the popular new television series,
Space Precinct novels follow a tough, street-smart
New York cop to the far corners of the galaxy.

Veteran NYPD Lieutenant Patrick Brogan
drew a wild card in the intergalactic Law
Enforcement Exchange program. He has moved
his entire family, including his ten-year-old
daughter Liz and his teenage son Matt, to the
planet Altor.

There are problems enough for a new family in
Altor's orbiting "space suburbs." But Brogan's
toughest job is down below, in the high-tech
slums of Demeter City, where alien species from
all over the galaxy—each with its own crime spe-
ciality—meet in a melting pot of mayhem and
murder!

Gerry Anderson's
SPACE PRECINCT

The Deity-Father
Demon Wing*

From HarperPrism

coming soon

ATTENTION: ORGANIZATIONS AND CORPORATIONS

Most HarperPaperbacks are available at special quantity discounts for bulk purchases for sales promotions, premiums, or fundraising. For information, please call or write:
Special Markets Department, HarperCollins Publishers,
10 East 53rd Street, New York, N.Y. 10022.
Telephone: (212) 207-7528. Fax: (212) 207-7222.

Gerry Anderson's

SPACE PRECINCT

THE DEITY-FATHER

DAVID BISCHOFF

HarperPrism
An Imprint of HarperPaperbacks

If you purchased this book without a cover, you should be aware that this book is stolen property. It was reported as "unsold and destroyed" to the publisher and neither the author nor the publisher has received any payment for this "stripped book."

This is a work of fiction. The charcaters, incidents, and dialogues are products of the author's imagination and are not to be construed as real. Any resemblence to actual events or persons, living or dead, is entirely coincidental.

HarperPaperbacks   *A Division of* HarperCollins*Publishers*
              10 East 53rd Street, New York, N.Y. 10022

Copyright © 1995 by Grove Television Enterprises
All rights reserved. No part of this book may be used or reproduced in any manner whatsoever without written permission of the publisher, except in the case of brief quotations embodied in critical articles and reviews. For information address HaperCollins*Publishers*, 10 East 53rd Street, New York, NY 10022.

Cover illustration © 1995 by Grove Television Enterprises

First HarperPaperbacks printing: July 1995

Printed in the United States of America

HarperPrism is an imprint of HarperPaperbacks. HarperPaperbacks, HarperPrism, and colophon are trademarks of HarperCollins*Publishers*

❖ 10 9 8 7 6 5 4 3 2 1

To John Silbersack

ACKNOWLEDGMENTS

THANKS TO
Jimmy Vines,
Grove TV . . .
And to Tom M. for
the Sicilian dialect.

SPACE PRECINCT
◆ THE DEITY-FATHER ◆

PROLOGUE

This crafty Creon was in the credits!

Yes sirree, Boboid, thought Haze Manarvan as dusk settled tight over Demeter City and the nightlife started blinking on in shades of neon and sin. *I'm in the money!*

The Creon whistled an old country drinking song to himself as he fairly skipped along the bustling avenue, back to work. What were the words? Tur-la-lee, tur-la-loo/Danny boy, I'm richer than you!

The being's huge eyes blinked and shone to either side of its head, like a pair of organic head-lights on eyestalks. The chunky humanoid body thumped along, breaking into a soft-shoe shuffle of glee from time to time, trailing a musky odor of the *darkan* brew he'd just drunk in his local tavern, patiently waiting for the sun to go down and the chrono-pieces to ding-dong the time he could head off to collect what he needed to get himself a pretty little piece of *ringching* from officers Brogan and Haldane. True, the payoffs for snooping around for those human police officers weren't princely sums. But they came regular with just normal informant duties (new hoods from Planet X moved down the block, kids doing a new kind of whack, that kinda stuff) and if he came up with something special, like this little number, he got himself a bonus. Yes, and with *that* moist piece, ol' Haze could stake himself in the big Zax game coming up. Haze always figured his problems with gambling were simple: he just never got enough money to stake himself proper. Deep pockets would do it; he was good with figures in his head, Haze was, and he just needed enough money to back him up until he got himself onto a winning streak. Then: watch out, Universe. Ol' Haze is ditchin' these pissant jobs he took, these lowlife informant duties he did for cops, shakin' this system's grim dust from his heels and headin' off for sun and surf at New Hawaii. Start choppin' the coconuts, start cookin' that whole pig, "Luau" Manarvan was on his way!

The factory took up a whole city block. It was tall and broad, and blocky, a Tarn-designed building that the Mrax Computer Systems had bought, gutted, then fitted out according to their needs and specifications. No Victorian chimneys belched smoke, no constant fires burned above chemical emissions—this wasn't that kind of factory. Nonetheless, call it what you like, thought

Haze, it was a sweatshop and he was sick of working there.

The normal street-sludge gave the place a wide berth, thanks to the bright halogens ringing the sides, the buzzing force perimeters, the antigrav robo-eyeballs bobbing along, guarding the perimeter. This was a tough neighborhood, and Mrax certainly didn't want any break-ins.

Haze waved his ID ring at the force perimeters and entered through the temporary break. He stepped up to the portal and stuck his face into the check-box. Retinal patterns determined. A microscopic bit of facial skin from a random part of his big head (sometimes they asked for a hand or even a foot, just for variety) was sliced off. With a chuff and a whir, DNA was analyzed, compared. Matched! A green light flashed and a gentle, friendly voice said, "Greetings, Worker Popxl 'Haze' Manarvan!"

"Greetings, Computer Personality Simulacrum!" said Haze. He could see data-flow flashing on a miniature screen: taking a voiceprint, just in case.

"Please. CIPS. Or just call me Maria, if you like."

This interchange happened every time; kind of like code phrasings. Mantras. And on the way out: benedictions.

"Havin' a good evening, Maria? Maintenance operations on line and all that stuff."

"Yes. Smooth running." Pause. Whir. Flash of light. "Worker Manarvan. You checked out over two hours ago, and there is no scheduling for your return until the day after tomorrow."

"Yeah, yeah, I know. I forgot to engage the lubrication filters on the Aisle Seven machine. If I don't kick that switch, some of tonight's maintenance ain't gonna be worth baxon droppings. Gonna have to do it all over again."

He'd done this on purpose, of course, so he'd have an excuse to come back now.

"Ah," said the computer. "Such a valuable fellow. Such should take approximately 16.5 minutes. Shall we expect you then?"

"Gimme a half hour point something. Got a craving for your pasta and meatballs in the commissary machines."

"Of course. They are delicious. Please be sure to purchase the ones seasoned for Creon tastes."

"Natch!"

A door opened.

Haze sauntered into the factory. "Ciao, baby."

"Ciao, Worker Manarvan."

The interior of the building was hollowed out, cavernous. Upper floors held offices. Down here were the light-splattered machines of this delicate industry, looking like a geometry-obsessed civilization's collision with Earthly Christmas. The place was deserted now, save for the maintenance machines: robots patrolling these banks of contraptions, checking this, oiling that, replacing something else. The place smelled of electricity, coolant, and that curious tinge unique to Mrax Computers, ever since Cost and Gnostra Industries took it over: a pervading aroma of tomato sauce and oregano from the commissary machines.

Haze's footsteps echoed as he padded heavily into the huge room. Whistling, he struck up another tune, in time with the oddly syncopated whooshing and clankings of robots: a damned curious but amusing symphony.

What Mrax produced in this place were more or less miniature computer circuit boards—only they were actually series of *micro* miniature computers, connected in series on boards. These in turn served as basic backup computer systems to thousands upon thousands of computers, from here on Demeter City to Earth and out past the Sirius system. This was new technology, and the boards were selling very well. There was already talk of adding another downtown factory . . . of expansion to space suburbs . . . other planets . . . This factory, in fact, had a sister back in Brooklyn, New York—Cost and Gnostra had in fact bought out Mrax Industries and adjusted their output as well as their cafeteria.

Haze toddled on past the machines, blithely dodging a squeaky little blip-runner robot, whipping around a corner and past the bulking, hulking machinery into his own little office cubicle.

There, on his desk, he found himself face-to-face with his own computer monitor and its hookups to the main systems. Still whistling, still dreaming of riches, still rattling those dice for the big "killing" in his head, he booted up. Hand on scanner for pawprint. Password filed, tap tap tap.

Graphics popped up on his monitor.

With practiced ease, he engaged the operations that would initiate the filtering system that he'd neglected, then keyed in a manual check for every five minutes. This procedure would authenticate the need for his presence here for some time.

Then he pulled out the computer cube that Officer Brogan had given him.

"An overlay vampire program," the Earther had said. "It will look for what we need. We can't get into the Mrax computer's systems. You can. Just pop this into your own computer, give the vampire fifteen minutes, and then go to the main control operations and copy what comes out there on a blank disk."

He slotted Brogan's cube in the drive, watched as new graphics danced onto his monitor. The policeman and his partner Haldane had assured him that this was the kind of program that could not be detected by the operating systems. It would merely observe the contents of its "host" computers, then take a few hasty "snapshots" and then unobtrusively dump out, leaving nary a sign that it had been anywhere near the area. Then all Haze would have to do was gather up the disk, tuck it into a pocket, and be on his larcenous way. The very idea of committing a misdeed in the interest of "law and order" was of great perverse appeal to the Creon.

Better yet, it could all occur while he treated himself to a veritable feast!

With a couple of taps, Haze "opened" up the access to the main computer. He grabbed a blank disk, and hopped over to the main control section, several dozen yards away. This would be viewed by monitors as perfectly normal—in order to get the filter instrumentation initiated, Haze had to throw a few knobs and switches here anyway.

At the main operations controls, Haze performed his maintenance duties. He slotted the two disks. Then he typed in the necessary commands that sent the "vamp" plunging on its merry way.

The rest was up to the programmers of truth, justice, and the Whatever way!

He looked around. No security robots were hovering, no Klaxons were sounding. Haze shrugged and grinned puckishly. Chowtime!

He hopped over a few robots and walked down to the end of the machine row, then angled down a hallway which shone and smelled with a new coat of wax.

Haze loved Demeter City, and he loved the exotic pieces of different worlds it brought him. He hadn't been born here; no, his family had emigrated from Danae when he'd been a feisty *marnk*-ager, eager for opportunity and trouble. Danae was a poor, mostly agricultural planet. Haze's family had worked on a farm, barely eking out sustenance from land overworked for millennia. The promise of Demeter City was the promise of both industry and a jumping-off point to the stars. Demeter City, on the planet Altor, after all, had been a twin project of hope on a planet uniquely situated near a jump point for intergalactic travel. It was a nexus of points from all parts of the known Universe, and it was here that a Creon could hope to rise above a destiny that might be termed sorry on his grim homeworld.

Haze strode into the commissary, heading immediately for the big central dispenser. He typed his ID in, palmed a plate, engaging his cred-account.

Near the wall, a floating eyeball focused on him.

Good. Security. Nothing amiss, here. Just a late-time worker having himself some vittles. It wasn't as though Worker Manarvan was drilling his way into the company safe. No, Worker Manarvan was just putting some of his pay back into the system.

He ordered up a request. Tapped his foot, whistling, as he waited. The machine flashed a light, a door opened, and there, in the recessed chamber, was a lovely dish holding a pile of ivory white spaghetti, topped with a rich thick tomato sauce and two mammoth, juicy meatballs.

"Mamma mia!" said the floating eyeball. "That's a spicy meatball."

Haze gave a thumbs-up sign. "You betcha. Faith, it is!"

Grinning, he took the steaming plate, grabbed himself a fork at the concession area, splashed on some grated Parmesan, a dash of oregano, and a heavy dusting of dried drool bugs.

Yum!

He took it to his cubicle and ate it, paging through a copy of Creon Mating Antics, occasionally looking up to check on the maintenance program he'd engaged, and generally lost himself in gustatory delight. These Cost and Gnostra guys sure knew how to cook!

When the filtering program was through, Haze regretfully twirled the last threads of pasta about the tines of his fork, mopped up some sauce, and ate it. Then he took the plate and licked the last dregs of sauce with his long, pimpled tongue.

Ah glory and begorrah! The Danaein duckfish urine was what gave the sauce its tart final kick Creons loved so much!

Then, dinner done, the Creon wandered over to see how that vampire program had done.

Everything looked just fine at the main station. The screen showed all maintenance couplings on-line, all programs running, everything just hunky-dory. All Haze had to do now was collect the cubes, pocket them, and be on his way for his late-night rendezvous with the Earther cop—after a few pints of stout at the tavern and a quick game of shell-cards, of course.

Press. Out popped the vampire cube.

Press. Out popped the storage cube.

No bells, no whistles. Easy as shooting dung-gas floaters in the boglands of home.

Haze was just starting to whistle again when the big screen started to change before him, attracting his attention.

Geometric designs and graphics morphed.

Collected into a face.

"Hey, dere, Haze. How dey hangin'?" said a cocky voice.

Haze Manarvan did a double take. He stared at the computer screen. The face was that of a skinny human with slicked-back hair, a long nose, a pencil mustache, and long sharp brows. Atop his head was a white hat, and he wore a dark suit with a red tie neatly positioned under a sharp chin. From a canted knife edge of a mouth, a burning cigarette tilted. In one lapel, the image-man wore a white carnation.

"Uh . . . pardon me? How are you?"

"Just call me Al, pal. Been watchin' you, guy. That pasta . . . watcha think. Good sauce, huh?"

"Delicious."

Geez! Just a monitoring program. Still, he'd never seen one like it before.

"Just like my old Sicilian gramma used to make, Haze. Say Haze . . . Hear you like to throw a little craps? Hear we won some of your salary back from you last week." The image scratched his nose, chewing something else in his mouth. "That's good. Keep it in the family, know what I mean?"

"Oh sure. I enjoy the games you guys put in this place. Very entertaining." Awkward pause. "Say, Al. You know, I'd better get going. Outside security kinda gave me a limit for being here and—"

Suddenly, the image in the computer pushed an arm through the glass interface. A silicon hand grabbed ahold of Haze's shirtfront, jerked him down toward the computer monitor. For the life of him, Haze could swear he smelled old garlic.

"And Haze. I also hear you been talkin' to that Brogan guy, huh? I also hear you been a stoolie. I also been watchin' you with those cubes. Not too bright, Haze. What do you think? Pretty stupid, huh?"

The eyes of the computer-image-made-solid glittered.

The jig was up. The Creon's spine froze.

However, Creons had the gift of gab, and Haze employed it now.

"What? Nonsense. I've been collectin' information, that's all. I'm just a free agent, Al. You want it, you got it. Tell you what. Bargain prices tonight. We could get a good one over on the cops, you bet. I could be a lot of use to you!"

"Not tonight, Haze. That's not the way we deal with betrayal to *this* particular company." A gust of cigarette smoke blew into Haze's face. He coughed and blinked. The next thing he knew, he was staring into the muzzle of a .38 Beretta.

"Uh, Hazy boy," said the computer-image-come-to-life. "Tonight . . . tonight you sleeps wit da fishoids."

The gun went off, and so did the back of the Creon's skull.

CHAPTER

It was Haldane who saw the dead Creon first.

He would have missed him, too, except that he was driving, and the body floated right up to the left of the brights of the police cruiser.

Brogan was looking at the chronometer, so he missed the sight initially. "Another five minutes, we stop circling and go down to the bar. I'm tired of waiting. This stuff is too damned important."

"Uhm—Brogan—" said Jack Haldane in a quiet, stunned voice.

Patrick Brogan drummed his fingers on the dashboard, impatiently. He was peering down into the spangled canyons of night that was the Phranx district, one of the rougher neighborhoods in Demeter City. He knocked back the dregs of his coffee, gearing his adrenaline up. Cops weren't real

David Bischoff

welcome in the Phranx. Brogan was a cop, and he'd
been in tough places before, plenty. He'd be in
many more, God willing, before he started cashing
his retirement checks. Each time, though, there
was always a price to pay. Brogan was just counting out his pennies.

He took a gulp of air, sighed it out. "I just hope
Jane Castle's right, and that program works.
Something damned weird is going on in this town
and I'm not going to be happy until I know what's
going on." He was a slender man with slicked-back,
blond hair and handsome chiseled face, and eyes as
blue as good china. Now his thin lips were bent in
a deep frown.

"Brogan, we've got a bogie at twelve o'clock
high," said Haldane. "And I don't mean Humphrey."

His partner gave Brogan a moment to look over
in the direction indicated and focus on the rising
object before he pulled up on the wheel and angled
the police cruiser up to keep pace. "You want to
shed some light, friend?"

Brogan flicked on a spotlight, adjusted it.

What he got was a light beam full of disheveled
clothing, dangling arms, and about three-quarters
of what used to be a Creon head. The Creon hung
upside down from two square blocks of what looked
like concrete, pulling him up toward the stars.

Blood dripped.

"I got a terrible feeling I know who that is," said
Haldane.

Brogan recognized what was left of the face. "I
just got a terrible feeling, period."

♦ 14 ♦

"Suggestions?"

Brogan stared for a moment at the ghostly apparition. "Well, we can't let him get to the police morgue on his own. Pull out the boat hook, snag him, and we'll tow him to a MechBase. Get some techs to torch off those shoes . . . "

"I'm going to scan him first. Might have a little booby trap for us boobies here."

"Took the words right out of my mouth. Been known to happen."

The beamer scan showed a pocket comb, some change, a Creon prophylactic, a picture of Mom, a wallet, a penknife, two antigrav boots bonded in psuedocrete, a dead Creon, no bomb. They didn't have the equipment to neutralize the antigravs, and they couldn't get to the controls because of the p-crete anyway. Fortunately, the antigravs weren't turned to max, so they'd be able to tow.

Haldane maneuvered. Brogan shot a grapple around the boots, cinched the line tight.

"Take it slow, guy," said Brogan. "We don't want to yank off the feet and have the poor guy tumble into someone's punch bowl." Brogan looked down at Demeter City, and thought of the nasty rich down there, the vicious poor. "Then again, maybe we do."

"I'll watch it, don't worry," said Haldane. Jack Haldane was a young guy, not much more than a rookie really. Handsome symmetrical face with a cute dimple and a twinkle in his eye below a sleek crop of black hair all the more astonishing in that it was his very own. He also happened to be just

about the best partner Patrick Brogan had ever
pulled. Funny, loyal, sharp. What the hell he was
doing on this armpit of a planet, Brogan could
never really figure out. Brogan had wanted a
change from New York. Hell, every New Yorker
wanted a change from New York. Haldane, though,
was too young for that. Maybe he'd come here so, if
he lived through the detail, he'd want a change
from Demeter City. Getting back to the Big Apple
would be a *treat* after Demeter City.

As the servos engaged, and the thrusters moved
the cruiser back to its way station here in the busi-
est place in the known civilized Universe, the two
partners were silent for a while.

Brogan thought about his wife and kids. Brogan
always thought about Sally and Matt and Liz when
he came upon a deader. This was what we all came
to: an inert and decomposing bag of flesh and
blood. He didn't want his family to get anywhere
near this kind of blunt truth about things. He
wanted to protect them, nurture them, keep them
pure. The truth was, Brogan not only dealt with
plenty of expediters of death. Patrick Brogan *was*
one. True, he was on the good side of the coin. But
he was on that coin, stamped there in blood. He
was a cop, and that was his job, and every time he
came home to the warmth and love of a good family
he knew the best of life. Still, he knew that it was
the best because he had his nose rubbed into the
worst almost every day.

And now they were towing some of the worst
right behind their hopper.

"I didn't know him," said Haldane, breaking the silence.

"Hmm? Haze Manarvan? A lowlife. He's not the big loss, the operation is." Too brusquely, too heartlessly.

Haldane thought about that for a moment. "I don't know. You're the one who scared him up off the streets, got him into our camp. And I don't remember you ever not laughing at his jokes and smiling after we saw him."

Silence.

Brooding silence at that.

"C'mon, Pat. It's been rough, I know, and let's face it, this is the roughest. You can talk about it if you want. You played shells with the guy, you had brews with him. You were worried about him. Now he's come up a corpse, and we're back to square one on the whole thing. Surely you've got something to say. Some kind of memorial epigram in memory of Haze Manarvan."

Brogan turned to his partner.

"Yeah. The son of a bitch owed me money."

He sank bank into his stewing darkness, and Haldane let him alone for the rest of the ride.

Captain Podly exploded.

"What?" he said, standing up from his desk, his Creon face reddening with rage.

Officers Brogan and Haldane stood, hats in hand, fingering them and eyeing each other in an "oh no" kind of way. Brogan was from a long line of

Irish cops, tracing his ancestry in America back to the nineteenth century potato famine. He always thought of the Irish as being the most Irish people in the Universe.

They weren't.

"You told me this operation would be a piece of cake!" yelled the burly Creon, his eyes blinking like some infuriated puppet's. He slapped a fist the size of a Ping-Pong paddle down on his desk. Paperweights wobbled, pens quivered. "Cake! Four informants dead, all involved with you two. Damned rotten and maggoty cake, if you'd be askin' me!"

The other occupants of the central room of the precinct couldn't help but turn their heads to observe the ruckus. For all Brogan knew, the outburst could be heard all the way down to Demeter City, above which this large space precinct hovered, a gigantic satellite perched in geosynchronous orbit. For the life of him, sometimes when things got like this, he could unfocus his eyes and the blur would be just like back home in Greater New York. Unfortunately, when he refocused, there would be Podly's big and unaesthetic red face, bellowing in front of him. The humanoid smelled of stale coffee and old cigars, and he'd had some onionlike substance for his latest meal.

Over in the corner, he could see Jane Castle swivel away and look like she was busy with something else entirely, totally oblivious to the tumult.

Unfortunately for Jane, her seat squeaked.

"Officer Castle!" bellowed Podly.

"Yes sir!" piped Castle in her sweet New Europe perky tones.

"Front and center, Castle!"

"Yes sir."

The young policewoman, looking fresh and spray-starched, stepped over and delicately took her place by Haldane. Officer Jack Haldane, in other circumstances, would have enjoyed the proximity. That Brogan knew for sure. Haldane clearly had an eye for the spritely Castle, and no wonder. Even though she affected a purely asexual pose generally in her simple pants and shirt uniform and discreet black faux-tie strip fronting all the blue, her hair pulled back into pure business mode, Castle couldn't hide that she was a beautiful woman. She had expressive eyebrows, sparkling green eyes, a pixieish nose, full pouty lips, smart chin, and model-high cheekbones. That she had a high amount of intelligence and a wit that could leap tall buildings at a single bound made her the most desirable human female this side of Ganymede.

Well, except for his wife, of course, and she didn't count because she was taken.

"Officer Castle," boomed Podly. "I understand that you've been involved in this operation as well."

"Yes sir. I'm supervising the vampire programs that we've been putting into use," she said.

"Seems that somebody may have put stakes into those programs' hearts, eh, Castle?" Podly leaned forward, chin stuck out in a Tell-Me-Anything-Else-I-Need-To-Know-Now pose.

"Sir . . . " said Haldane. "We don't know that for sure. We don't know anything for sure."

"That's right, Podly," said Brogan, rallying to the defense. "We're doing our best down there. In normal circumstances, these things would have been slick as Nargarina bat guano. It's not normal, though. That's the problem."

Podly stared at them for a moment, his two protruding eyes blinking with frustration. Then he just sighed and sank down in his chair, placing his big head into his big hands.

"You know, when my old Sergeant Nogle took me down on my first beat, he took me into a *narla* parlor and bought me a cup of the steamin' stuff. And he says, 'Podly, me boy. Rule Number Two—Rule Number One bein' watch your back—Cultivate yourself good informants. You don't have informants down in the mean streets of Demeter City, you don't have squat.' When you two came here, we had an army of fine, healthy squealers, we had a digit on the erratic pulse of this sick city. In the past two weeks, we've lost four of 'em—and they all were associated with the three of you. Talk to me, people. And let's try and make some sense out of this sorry situation."

Brogan nodded. At least the temper tantrum had abated. "Maybe it would be a good idea if we review the situation."

Podly nodded. "That would be a fine idea." He gestured toward chairs. "Rest your brains, gentle beings. That's sure what I'm doing with mine."

The trio took their seats. Podly slid out a control panel and hit a button that grew a privacy bubble around the conference.

Then those two strange eyes focused on Brogan, silently voicing a stereoscopic "Well?"

Brogan whipped a glance at both Castle and Haldane that said "Feel free to jump in at any time," then proceeded.

"I smell some kind of crime syndicate brewing, Podly," he said.

"Yes. You've said as much before," said the Creon. "We've got plenty of organized crime. Little fiefdoms, big fiefdoms. It's a tradition in Demeter City. They come, they go. We smash them, they smash themselves. One envelops another. Faith! I remember one group tried to buy me when I was on my beat. When I got this desk, I put the lot of 'em in the slammer."

"Like I've been trying to convince you, Podly, this isn't nickel-and-dime stuff here. This isn't extortion or rackets or gambling or vice—though all those things are like satellites, I suppose." He shook his head. "I'm a student of these kinds of things, and I dealt with a *real* mob back home on Earth. I sense an intelligence working through these little gangs down on Demeter. I sense a coalition growing, I sense a power forming."

"Brogan's right," said Haldane. "I haven't got his years of experience, but I've got eyes and ears. When I got the basic cop course on Demeter, I thought 'Chaotic Crime.' I mean, you've got a little of everything down there, Podly . . . things we've never heard of on Earth. A Universe of crime. But it's all jumbled up." He nodded. "Someone . . . or something . . . is weaving the threads together. I'm just hoping it's not a shroud for law enforcement."

"Pah!" said Podly. "You two . . . Of course there're criminals down there, of course there're ganglords. They come, they go. We kick 'em out, we incarcerate 'em, we kill 'em. That's our job. We're cops. Me, I'm just wondering if you're not looking at normal Demeter City underworld activity and using the wrong procedures . . . I'm thinkin' that's why these informants are getting themselves planted." He leaned over and glared at Officer Castle. "Castle, you've been here longer than these Earthworms. What's your take?"

Castle took a breath, then launched. "Well, sir, I must say I, too, see this as yet another anomaly in a center for anomalies—"

"Speak plainly, dammit!"

"I mean, I agree with you . . . "

Podly leaned back, smiling.

" . . . to a certain extent. Demeter City is a hotbed of crime. All flavors. However, albeit there seem to be a number of traditional elements here— including the unfortunate demise of informants— what's unusual isn't just the clump of coincidence of these deaths. It's the nature of the crimes we're investigating."

"Gentlemen—would you translate for this sorry illiterate flatfoot!" said Podly, not sure if he were being complimented or slammed.

"What Jane means is this is high-tech stuff we're looking at here," Haldane blurted.

"Along with some very odd low-tech," added Brogan. His stomach was growling, and he felt uncomfortable. He hated these privacy bubbles. For some reason, they gave him a headache, and he felt one coming on now.

"High-tech? Wake up and smell the Universe, people. You're in the future here! You Earthies took a hell of a jump into ultra-tech. We're talkin' FTL, we're talking stuff I sure don't understand. I know enough for my job. I know the low-tech stuff, though, you bet, and there ain't nothing I ain't seen on Demeter's streets . . . and stuff you sure ain't seen yet."

Podly seemed to have a bug up his lower intestines about this, and Brogan sensed why. Podly hated to be out of control, and he *too* sensed something, deep down, something that he didn't like and was trying to deny. In a way, he was just hashing this out. He was trying to get Brogan and company to convince him.

Brogan needed some aspirin.

Brogan jumped to the challenge presented.

"Podly, if you take us off this, you'd be making the mistake of your career. Castle's right. We're talking crime in high places. Crime among factory and corporation owners that stretches from the gutters to the stars. . . . I've been a cop for over twenty years, and I've got a gut sense for these things. We're onto something, and that something knows it. That's why we've got four dead informants."

Podly stroked his chin. Made a dismissive gesture. "Pah! You think I'd take my best people off something important." He smiled grimly. "Just stirrin' the peat here, Brogan. Now, let's get down to brass tacks. We've got dead informants on our hands. This last guy apparently got caught with his hand in the computer cookie jar, so to speak."

"Yes, that's near as we can guess," said Castle, chin up bravely. "I can't understand it, really. The program was supposed to be foolproof, untraceable."

"And the other informants . . . Snick Dergil, I think, was the first." Podly consulted a list. "A rather lecherous old Tarn."

"Garrotted," said Haldane, helpfully.

"We had him on detail at one of the numbers rackets," Brogan said. "He's the one who first noticed some of the same people at different places."

"Then Jerg Norvik . . . disintegrated?"

"Yeah. Dock duty, checking for contraband," said Brogan.

"We're pretty sure a spaceship landed on him," said Haldane.

"Ah. Probably dead first, then, eh?" said Podly. His thick finger slipped down to the next name. "Hargill Fafall . . . " Sorrowful shake of his head. "Cripes, I remember this guy from the Old Creon's Gentlemen's Club. Well connected with the infamous. One of our very best . . ."

"He's a Jimmy Hoffa," said Haldane. "We're pretty sure he's part of the foundation of some building now."

"All right, then," said Podly. "Facts. Then theories."

Castle and Haldane turned to Brogan expectantly yet leerily and Brogan knew why. Podly wasn't going to like this theory at all.

"It's the Mob," said Brogan.

"Oh, that's hopeful. Of course it's a mob. A collection of criminals, with a hierarchal structure. Real insightful, Brogan. You get an extra donut at dinner."

Brogan shook his head. "You don't understand. Not just any old Demeter crime ring. Not just your average intergalactic group of thugs. I'm talking the genuine article, the Mob. The Mafia. Direct from Earth by way of Sicily, the United States, and the twentieth century."

Podly's eyes got bigger than Brogan had ever seen them before. "Nonsense."

"I know it seems impossible," said Brogan, "but I see earmarks. There could be just imitation of methodology here, but you have to remember—I dealt with Mob members on Earth."

Haldane shook his head. "I know my criminal history, and I can understand your incredulity, Podly. I wasn't sure myself—I've only read about the Mafia. But when I saw those cement galoshes . . . Well, it's warped, but it's a possibility."

"I know my Earth history as well," said Jane Castle. "Organized crime that could trace its origins back to the arrival of Sicilian and Italian families on Ellis Island during the great immigrations of the late nineteenth century and early twentieth century was removed as an infrasocial problem by Earth governments ten years ago, the criminals effectively either jailed or reprogrammed. This, of course, did not end organized crime—only the more obvious sorts." She smiled faintly. "Neither Haldane nor I have had any immediate experience of the personalities involved with this sort of crime style. Brogan has. I'm a fact-oriented person, Podly. But when it comes to experience and hunches, I think I'll throw my lot in with Brogan's ideas. He's been pretty much dead-on in the past."

"I don't know," said Podly. "This is a wild corner of the Universe. We grow wild, we import wild . . . . But the Mob? From Earth? That's hard for me to swallow."

Brogan clapped his hands together. "Shall we trot out the little factoid, folks?"

"I guess we'd better. Jane?"

Jane Castle pursed her lips, and pulled out a computer printout. Handed it to Podly.

Podly wrinkled it in his heavy hands, staring down at the densely typed paper, looking bemused. "So. What is this nonsense?"

"I did a computer search on the owners of all the businesses we've been trying to investigate. They're all owned by one corporation, a corporation that just arrived on Demeter last year." She leaned over and tapped a line. "That's the name."

Podly peered down. "Cost and Gnostra?"

"A play on the Sicilian," said Brogan. "Cosa Nostra. 'Our Thing.'"

"Criminey, people. You're saying that these jokers are the Mob and waving red flags in our faces?"

"I don't need a spectrometer to detect red," said Brogan.

"I don't need a pole to see a flag," said Haldane.

"And the Cost and Gnostra, sir. . . I can trace it from Earth," said Castle.

"What else can you trace, Castle?"

"I'm working on it, sir."

Podly tapped his thick fingers on the desk. "Well then. I see we've got quite a kettle brewing here. I'm still not convinced it's anything like you say it is. You ask me, the human brain is *born* addled. But I'm not the kind of cop who can say another cop's hunches are nonsense. I've *survived* because of gut feelings before." He stood up, looking tall and magnificent and totally in charge. "Right. I'm not taking you off this, I'm going to put you in deeper. Castle, you just keep on tracing and computer analyzing and what you do."

"Yes sir."

"Brogan and Haldane . . . sounds like you two should have a look at this Mrax Industries. An employee has turned up dead. Grounds for a search warrant, I think. A *deep* search warrant." He turned to the woman. "I want you to go with them. Take whatever programs or equipment necessary to go through their computer systems."

"Great!" said Haldane. "Good call, sir."

Podly glared at him. "Brogan, this sound okay to you?"

"A little brusque and blatant, maybe."

"The sneaky way got four informants killed, Brogan," said Podly, leaning on his desk with all the gravity of his authority. "No, Brogan. If the Mob is out there, they know by now that we're onto them."

Brogan nodded. Podly was right.

The odd thing, though, was that if indeed his worst suspicions were true, and remnants of organized crime from Earth had somehow resurrected themselves and translated themselves into Demeter City . . . .

Why?

And why did the Mob seem to *want* the Cops to know?

CHAPTER

At the top of the skyscraper, the man stood by the window of his palatial office, gazing down across the cityscape.

The man wore an elegant dinner jacket. His hair was short and neatly clipped, gleaming with the pomade he used to keep it down. In his hand he held an ivory cigarette holder. The delicious aroma of illegal tobacco twirled up, like a simple DNA lattice.

The entirety of the huge office was done in art deco style, right down to the fireplace, where real oak burned, sizzling and cracking with merry flame. The place even smelled of Earthly smells, circa the late 1930s, despite the fact that it was not just many years, but many light-years, distant in time and space.

"Mine," whispered the man. "Soon mine."

A tinkling of a bell.

The elegant handsome man turned.

An alien crawled in.

It looked like an octopus on legs. It wore a cape, triple-lensed spectacles. It smelled of distant biomes.

On its head was perched a roadster's cap.

"Well?" said the slender, elegant man.

"They took the bait." The translator the alien wore on a little sashed belt wheezed and slurred the words in odd places.

"Brogan and Haldane?"

"Yes." The affirmative came out Yessssssss, like a message from some Lovecraftian creature.

"And they took the body back to their accursed armed satellite?"

"Yes. For the autopsy as you predicted."

The elegant, dark man drew on his cigarette holder. "Excellent. You have done well, Licknose."

The alien bowed. His tentacles—on closer inspection much rougher and certainly hairier than those of his early underwater counterpart—seemed to preen.

"This works well. They, of course, have little hope of finding the little surprises that we injected into the body of the Creon."

"No. Hardly."

"And they thought they were clever with a new-fangled—or should I say 'new-fanged'—vampire program. Pah!"

"Pah!" mimicked the alien, shaking with what could either be laughter or some kind of odd epileptic seizure.

"Well then. That stage is under way. Now for the subsidiary plan. However, I believe we have time for a quick game."

The set of eyes behind the wired lenses gleamed with anticipation. "Good. Perhaps I shall win this time!"

The elegant man went to a desk, where he sat down. He opened a drawer and pulled out a deck of playing cards.

The alien wobbled up to the desk. Four tentacles lengthened, broadened, and settled into a chair, upon which the creature placed its torso. Two tentacles grew through the creature's chartreuse surplice. The knobby ends grew digits with opposable thumbs, only vaguely resembling human hands but serving the same function.

The alien called Licknose (a phonetic approximation of his true name in his own tongue—or whatever its analogous organ was) leaned forward intently.

The elegant gentleman shuffled the cards. He slowly began to deal.

"There are various levels of enjoyment and satisfaction I'm having here on this planet, you know, Licknose."

"I've only just learned the game of gin! You shouldn't take so much satisfaction in beating me!" said the alien.

"What? This? No, just a trifle. And you'll beat me eventually." A slip, a slap of cards. "No, I mean of my operation on Demeter City. I'm here for more reasons than one."

"Ah yes. You mentioned a van ditty or some sort?"

The eyes eagerly ogled the descending cards.

"Vendetta, Licknose. Vendetta."

"Ah yes. Against that officer. Brogan, I think."

"Yes. Brogan. The *mamaluke*. I have a quite interesting way to deal with Patrick Brogan," said the elegant gentleman, putting down the final card, then placing the stack of remainders between them. "A way of savoring his fall, his demise, his destruction."

"Most fascinating."

"But you know, this is more than a vendetta. My people perhaps would not approve of my vengeance. Patrick Brogan, the *gavon* has a family, you know."

"Egglings? A brood cow?"

"Something along those lines. Only less disposable I think. It will cause Brogan a great deal of pain to lose his family. But before very long . . . they will belong to me."

"Ah!"

"I have already set things in motion on that account. A most devious and clever plan, I think."

"You are a most fascinating being, Dominick Monteleone."

Monteleone nodded, basking in this praise from bizarre and distant star shores.

"Before we begin, Licknose . . . I've been meaning to ask you. You are the only individual of your race I have encountered on Demeter City. And yet, you've proved to be of the most use . . . both as a colleague and as a friend."

The alien let that filter through his translation device for a moment.

"Thank you."

"Is there anything else that you are in this for besides riches, power, domination of this planet . . . and perhaps other planets . . . no, even this galaxy?"

"Actually, yes," said the alien. "I want you to help kill my mother."

Dominick Monteleone smiled.

"And your *nona* as well?"

"What?"

"The Sicilian word for 'grandmother'."

"Sure. Why not?"

"I believe that can be arranged."

Putting his cigarette holder back in his mouth and taking a puff, he turned over the card atop the deck.

It was the queen of spades.

CHAPTER

It was a Saturday
morning of the very worst kind when the package
from N'ninoct Simulations, secret subsidiary of
Cost & Gnostra, came for Matt Brogan.

"Hi," said the package. "You sent for me."

"You bet I did!" said the teenager, grabbing the
thing from the delivery Tarn and signing for it.

Brogan was sitting at the kitchen table, feeling as droopy as his robe, drinking a cup of coffee as this scene took place. It wasn't a very
good Saturday morning because Brogan knew
that he was going to have a shift coming up in
the afternoon, a special shift that was going to
be a doozy, kicking off this onerous investigation. Brogan had just managed to drag himself
out of bed in order to enjoy a morning of family

time, and frankly, just between his cup of java and him, he would have preferred to be back communing with his pillows.

"Wait a minute," he said, getting up and walking to the door. "What do you have there, Matt?"

"Molten new game for the box, vox!" said the fourteen-year-old, eyes afire with enthusiasm. "It'll lay tracks down your spine."

"Whoa there . . . " He looked at the Tarn. "Did you check this?"

"Yes sir. Of course!" The slender nervous creature looked as though he was about to open his third eye with alarm. "We check all incoming mail material, particularly packages. We are well aware of the sensitive position of your status here in our society. This is why you and your family live here in the suburbs. There are those down below on Demeter City who, alas, would do you harm."

"Well, I don't mean to be paranoid, but sometimes that's very true. So you analyzed this."

"Yes. It's just as the youngster claims. A computer cube containing a three-dimensional sim game involving propulsionary devices to—"

"Right, right, I can pretty much guess that part of it . . ."

"No bombs, no bugs, viruses, or other computer diseases." The Tarn cocked his wattled head. "Nothing of harm that either our devices or my additional senses can detect."

"Thanks. Sorry. Just checking."

"And well you should. However, be assured, we do our very best here to assure that no harm comes to the denizens of this complex. Particularly citizens of your value and stature."

The Tarn bowed and departed.

"Yaks, Dad! You've been watching too many secret-agent shows!" said Matt. Eagerly he was opening the package.

"Ouch!" said the package. "Please do not manhandle. Delicate equipment inside."

"Oh dear," said Sally Brogan, Matt's wife, as she walked in from the patio. She carried a potted plant, a trowel, and wore a scuff of dirt on her cheek. "Another anthropomorphized object. These Demeter companies do seem to go for that."

Matt raised an eyebrow. "Don't you mean xenopomorphized, Mom?" He was examining a printout of instructions that had been included with the pack. He was a good-looking guy with brown hair and wry eyes. Every time Matt looked at her, Brogan could see his mother in him—and his amusing rebellion. That's what kids his age did. Break off, form their own identities, be gigantic and annoying pains. Matt's trouble was that he couldn't help but be lovable, even through all this pubescent change, and it drove the boy nuts.

"Whatever. I feel like I'm in Toontown at times," said Sally, giving a weary smile. "Hey, big guy," she said to her husband. "Save some of that coffee for me. I'm in need of a serious fix."

"Me too. How about a dirty hug first." Brogan got two armfuls of her. The familiar soft and female sensations, around a bedrock of personality and character. She smelled of dirt and shampoo and Sally, and it made him relax somewhat after his concern about the package.

"Toons! Toons! I love Toons!" said Liz, their eleven-year-old as she skipped into the room. "Surround me with Toons! Drown me with Toons. Hound me with Toons!" She was pretty and sweet, Liz was, with girlish character and a hyperactive mind that pinballed around the Universe. Curious, alive. Her eyes were like Brogan's, only they hadn't seen the things a twenty-five-year veteran cop had seen. They were innocent and full of mischief.

"Send in the Loons!" said Matt, rolling his eyes with melodramatic disgust. He fixed Liz with a look of mock contempt. "Oh. Don't bother. One's here."

"Stephen Sondheim. Paraphrase!" said Liz, going into her psuedosophisticate mode.

Geez, thought Brogan. *These kids absorb culture like a barfly absorbs liquor. And they get just as drunk on it.*

"So. New game, Matt?" said Liz. "Can I play? Can I, can I, can I?"

"Game!" replied the package. "I am no game. I am a entertainment and educational environment. I may be diverting, but I am no mere game."

"Where'd you get it?" Liz wanted to know.

"More to the point, where did you get the money for it?" said Sally. "You quit your part-time job because of the heavy school year workload, if I recall, and I don't see you saving your allowance for something like this."

Matt looked as though he was being put through something so tedious he could barely stay awake. "Third-degree time. Well, in case you may not have noticed it, I'm not only doing okay in school . . . I'm being scrutinized by computer companies."

"Oh?" said Brogan. "Care to elaborate?"

"Sure. It's simple. They found out that I'm from Earth, and I've got certain mouth-watering demographic appeal. I'm young, handsome, intelligent—and a genius at the keyboard."

"With smelly socks, a new jockstrap, and a crush on Margill Toesy!" said Liz, giggling.

Margill Toesy was the star of the most popular show on Earth TV, an evening soap they had to import for Matt and Liz to watch. Kids in high school, doing kids-in-high-school things. Toesy was the teen dream of the show, with blond hair and an incredible figure and the personality of a sexy leprechaun. Hell, Brogan had a crush on Margill . . . Any testosterone within laser shot of those green eyes couldn't help but be affected.

Matt, however, blushed.

"Gimme a break, sister. I'm in an awkward stage of my sexual development!"

"I'll say!" chuckled Liz. "I heard you tried to kiss Amy Nardo the other day and she said it was *extremely* awkward."

"Liz!" said Sally, sharply trying to hide her own interest and amusement. "You know there's a thing called karma. One day this kind of teasing is not going to sit well with you."

David Bischoff

Matt, crimson, tried to change the subject back to things more in his control.

"Anyway, so some of these companies really want to be part of the *huge* Earth market. Who am I, but the perfect test guy. I get this stuff *free* . . . all I have to do is play . . ."

"Please!" said the package stiffly.

"Er . . . that is, experience the program's modular component interworking effect on my . . . uhm . . ."

"What the young man is trying to say," said the package, "is that we at N'ninoct Simulations are presenting him with this program in the hopes of learning the proper integration methodology for adolescent human minds. In return, we supply not merely 'full cool' prestige for young Matthew, occupying his time with 'far radical' devices, clever hand-eye coordination engagements, we educate him in thinking parameters and modes that will aid him with possible contact with extraterrestrial creatures."

"Well that's very nice to know," said Sally. "Question is, can you fix his horrendous spelling?"

"Aw, Mom! You're embarrassing me!"

"I'm sorry. We are not programmed for remedial English tutorials. This, simply, is not our province," said the package. "Please forgive the limits of this AI prospective tester interface; however, may I say in answer to your misgivings that it is an honor to work with your species, and N'ninoct Sims and we humbly entreat allowance of your youngling to enjoy our product."

"Oh cripes!" said Matt. "You're not going to

make me send it back, are you? I mean, when I checked off YES on that letter I just figured you'd want me to . . . you know . . . grow galactically intellectual. I mean, as long as I'm so far away from Earth, I might as well make the most of it."

"I'm not sure if I'm real thrilled with being a test market here, guy," said Brogan.

"I don't really see the harm," said Sally. "And he's right. That's one of the reasons we signed up. To give the kids a chance to grow in ways other kids don't."

"You bet. Matt wants to move beyond Earthly Nerd straight to Galactic Geek!" said Liz.

"And Liz wants to move from age eleven straight to the Afterlife!" said Matt, balling up a fist.

Liz stuck out her tongue defiantly.

"Whoa! Whoa!" said Brogan, moving between the two of them. Generally the two got along fine, but every once in a while sibling rivalry or sheer sister/brother antipathy got the best of them. Sally assured him it was perfectly normal, and he could well remember getting into scuffles with his big brothers when he was a kid. Still, he knew what his role as father was here. Keep them from killing each other. "Now what's going on here? Liz, why are you giving your brother such monumental grief?"

"It's simple," said Matt. "She's not as smart as I am, and she *knows* it. She'll never have my talents. I'm going to achieve far more than her with my life, in style and class, and she's going to be lagging in my dust her whole life!"

Liz looked as though she'd been slapped in the

face. Her stunned expression dissolved into tears. She ran for the bedroom, crying.

"Oh, great. Thanks, guy. You're real good for her self-esteem," said Brogan, grabbing his son by the shoulder and giving him the hairy eyeball.

Matt was incensed. "*Her* self-esteem. She's the one who's attacking *me*. I'm sorry, but she's been on my case ever since we did those IQ Depth tests and I came out *far* ahead of her!"

He wasn't giving an inch and he looked about as willing to apologize or cave in as a hormone-driven statue. The old Irish in Brogan wanted to bend the willful boy over one knee and hand-thunder some respect into him. However, his father had done that to him, and it still hurt. He'd resolved never to put *his* son through that. He trotted out the old-fashioned number count, cooled down a few degrees, then turned to his wife.

"You want to go talk to Liz?"

"I will later, but she's got to start learning some boundaries herself," said Sally. "I'm not saying that either of these bright brats are right. I'm just saying that we're going to have to figure out some other solution than molly-coddling them."

"All I wanted was a little relaxation this morning," said Brogan. "That's all. I've got a hard shift this afternoon and evening."

Matt slapped his forehead. "Drag! Does this mean that you're going to punish me for being smart and taking opportunities for intergalactic intellectual advancement! Does this mean that you're not gonna let me use the sim?"

"That, sir, would indeed be a tragedy!" insisted the package. "And I have not yet mentioned the possible scholarship involved."

Scholarship. That word gave Brogan pause. A cop didn't make much. His father had been a cop, and Brogan had gone to Columbia University majoring in criminology anyway . . . but only at the cost of a lot of sacrifices by his parents and himself . . . He'd ended up a cop anyway, because of economics. He'd always wanted his son to have a chance at the very best. A chance to get what he wanted from life. He and Sally were saving up, but with the incredible costs of the very best universities these days, there would probably be problems. A cop didn't make fistfuls of money—not even a cop in Demeter City at the center of the known Universe. A lot of money filtered through, sure. A cop lives on his salary and benefits, period. An honest cop not on the take, anyway. And if nothing else, Patrick Brogan prided himself on being an honest cop.

"Careful," he said. "There are laws against attempting to bribe a policeman."

"Ah, c'mon, Dad. Remove the plank from the posterior!" said Matt. "This is on the up-and-up!"

"Not to worry, young Matt!" piped the package. "Everything about our programs, from the questionnaire onward fully complies with the intersection of all laws on and above Demeter City. And the scholarship is only a possibility. Its issuance and its levels depend entirely upon both aptitude and performance."

"Okay, okay," said Brogan, dismissing the pair of them. "Go fool with your sim to your heart's content. I don't want two teary kids today."

"Hey! Thanks, Dad. Come on, guy." He tucked the package under his arm.

"Many congratulations, Mister Brogan," said the package as Matt retreated. "You have made a wise decision. May I also transmit a suggestion to headquarters to enter your name to test-market our more adult products?"

"No thanks," said Brogan.

He grumped back to the kitchen and poured himself some more coffee. He felt his wife starting to rub his back and he turned to her.

"Hey there, kiddo. Want some?" He scooped her up and planted a kiss on her cheek.

"Thanks."

He poured a new cup, added milk.

This was a precious ritual with them. Coffee. Companionable, stimulating, intense yet relaxed. With your mouth wrapped around the smooth, unique liquid and its dance on your adrenals, the smell of company, the feel. At these times, he could just close his eyes and pretend they were back in their roomy row house in Brooklyn, with a Sunday and *The New York Times* stretched before them like the landscape of heaven.

He missed that part of New York, but he still could get that kind of contentment out of the quiet time with Sally. She was big-time wonderful, and never, for a single second, did he forget that fact.

"Well. So much for a family Saturday morning,"

he said. "You'd think they'd cling to the old man when he's around. A piece of home. Far as I can tell those two have pretty much adapted."

"For the most part. Don't worry about Liz. I'll check on her in a minute. Me, I think *you're* the one that needs attention at the moment."

They sat down on the couch, falling into a comfortable, companionable assembly of arms and legs and robe. Brogan sipped his coffee, savoring it and her. "You've got a rough assignment coming up. I can always tell. Want to talk about it?"

"Sure. Eventually. Let's just talk about small stuff first, okay. The right brain needs a little vacation."

"What about the left brain."

"It's a total burnout."

She laughed. "Okay."

So they talked about the things she was involved in. Brogan could never understood why some guys weren't interested in the lives their wives led when they were at work. Maybe it was just that Sally had such a gift for language, maybe she just made it all fascinating . . . or maybe it was just that he was simply very absorbed with her. Certainly it was a wonderful change from patrolling a tough city, dealing with vice, homicide, and criminals and the unsavory things he had to deal with.

He listened as she talked about her gardening, the kids, the various seminars about Earth culture she led here, the tour groups she was involved with, the classes she took herself in understanding

their intergalactic neighbors. Not to mention her
job as a post-trauma therapist. She was even
starting to even master a couple of alien languages. In truth, Brogan suspected that he'd been
chosen as one of the exchange cops on Demeter not
just because he was a good cop, but because of
Sally and the kids. They were involved with all
kinds of programs and theoretically made a perfect model Earth nuclear family to show off to the
galaxy. . . .

Well, good thing nobody was watching this
morning . . .

He listened to Sally, sipping his coffee and relaxing, and a little voice at the back of his head woke
up and asked that annoying little question as it did
sometimes.

*Hey Brogan. How did you and yours end up
becoming the twisted Jetsons of Demeter City?*

Damned good question, actually.

When the Galactic Council had contacted Earth
and announced to the New United Nations that
the planet had reached a level of sophistication in
civilization sufficient to be allowed to join the
Great Big Cosmic Party, so to speak, Brogan's had
been one of the billions of minds to bask in the
awe of First Contact. The stars were opening—
knowledge and beauty and completion surely
awaited.

However, after the Tarns who made the contact
completed their diplomatic mission, making every
news report, every magazine cover, every paper in
the world (especially those incredible third eyes), and

left behind a wealth of educational materials, promising future diplomatic missions, Brogan began to study the facts about the Universe. Although he too found a sense of wonder as the scientists and top minds did in the network of worlds that the elegant and peaceful-looking Tarns had revealed to Earth, and the strange things the Universe had to offer once one slipped the bonds of the Sol system, there was one curious fact that kept on getting under-lined in his head when he studied the actual civi-lizations involved:

The Universe, basically, was business as usual.

Technological civilizations throughout the galaxy oddly mirrored the technological civiliza-tions that had grown on Earth. In some ways, in fact, Earth civilization by the middle of the twenty-first century had worked some things out better than any other civilization.

Which was maybe why other civilizations were interested and thought maybe it wouldn't be a bad idea to get these human beings out into the galaxy.

Odd. A lot of philosophers of the twentieth cen-tury had suggested that mankind's egregious his-tory perhaps meant humans were unfit to populate the Universe. Now, rather than the dregs as had been suspected, they were considered something of the cream. Good examples. Teachers, potential friends, helpers.

At first, Brogan just got on with his cop life, doing what he did best on the complex and hard streets of New York City. When the exchange pro-gram started, and cops started to volunteer to go and help out at this, the Crime Capital of the Universe, Demeter City, Brogan had scoffed.

Years later, though, when his aptitude test for such work got high marks, and the kids started growing and exhibiting fascination with xeno-subjects and his wife's intelligence began to flower beyond the family into other areas, Brogan began to realize that he was being close-minded and selfish. Besides, truth was that the same-old, same-old was getting to him. He found himself in a midlife crisis, and the thing he needed to give him a fresh outlook on life, he realized, was a change.

Of course, this wasn't just a sea change . . .

It was an intergalactic space change . . .

And it had been, Brogan knew instinctively, the *right* change.

Oh, there had been a few bumps, and life could often get on the roller coaster here. But the experience, in general, was just amazing. He was not only having a rewarding life . . . He felt he honestly made a difference down there in Demeter. In New York, sometimes you could get overwhelmed by the hardness of all the crime and the amount of it. In Demeter City, bigger than New York, possibly more dangerous, he could actually see what his work and knowledge and experience were doing for the place . . . and thus, for the Universe.

Besides, he got a boost in salary . . .

Besides, *The Jetsons* was his favorite twentieth-century cartoon.

When he finished his coffee and kissed his wife,

Brogan said, "You know, maybe we'd better see about Liz."

"She'll be all right."

"I'm sure, but I'm not quite so adept with day-to-day stuff with the kids and I'd feel a lot better if I talked with her."

"Just don't encourage her present behavior."

"If I had time, I'd have a little family powwow. I don't, though. Anything look likely on the schedule?"

"Next Saturday morning I think. I'll line the kids up. Should I drill holes in the paddle?"

"Uhm . . . . That would sting my poor rear end far too much."

She laughed. "So what's going on downtown?"

He shook his head. "We're investigating an operation that's cost us four informants. Looks like we've got some organized crime moving in."

She grew a little more serious. "Well, that's certainly right up your alley, isn't it? I mean, you've dealt with it before."

"Yes, and I need a stomach antacid for this one."

"A little bit queasy?"

"Uh-huh. Either an antacid or a butterfly net."

"Go on."

"I'm getting a bad feeling about this one. Can't put my finger on it."

"Well, keep me informed. If you ever need to talk . . . " She tapped her head. "Remember, I've got the complete case files of Officer Patrick Brogan right here, in his own words and reactions."

"Yes, you do, don't you?" He kissed her. "Let me think about it. I'll get back to you tonight."

"Oh! Kinky pillow talk!"

"Only the very best for my baby."

A squeeze, and he was up. Stretch. Creak.

"Sounds like you're going to need a little massage tonight, too."

"Hmmm! Something to live for." He moved his neck around. "I've got a racquetball game set with Haldane before we go out. That and a hot shower, and I think I'll be okay. Anyway, I can always apply for new body parts."

"Just make sure you check with me first before you make any significant exchanges."

He chuckled and made his way to speak to his daughter.

He looked in for a moment through the open door of his son's room. A gigantic hologram of a dopey-looking dragon-thing was hovering above his computer, picking its nose and discoursing on some obscure character point concerning some adventure in progress. Not a game. Right. He sighed heavily and made his way to his daughter's room.

She had a poster of a fairy princess displayed, smiling and waving a wand in blessing upon all creation.

Rapped lightly.

"Hey, princess. You okay?"

The life-size eyes of the picture-princess suddenly came alive. They stared down upon him imperiously.

"Who goes there!"

"Me, pumpkin!" he said, slightly alarmed. This was new.

"How do I know it's not some horrid troll, disguised as my trollish father?"

"Uhm . . . well, I was actually going to leave Mr. Hyde outside and have Dr. Jekyll make a bedside visit."

Optical fibers in the wand shifted. Suddenly the implement of magic became a shining sword, gleaming three-dim from the two-dim environment.

"Enter. Make a false move, however, vassal . . . And snicker snack! Off with your head!"

The door opened of its own accord.

Brogan walked into the room.

The place was well lit and covered with pictures and books and dolls and stuffed animals; a very little-girlish environment, with several high-tech elements thrown in. A 3-D set, a computer . . .

And a Virtual Reality headset and gear on his sweet flesh and blood, with which she had controlled the little show on the door, with which she was experiencing, doubtless, her own little fantasy world.

She pulled the goggles off and sat up, regarding her father. Tears had long since dried from her eyes. "Hi."

"Hi to you. Just checking to make sure you're okay."

"Is the Geek still alive?"

"Last time I checked."

"Then I'm *not* okay."

He went to her bed, sat down. "Sounds bad."

"It's *terrible*."

"I'm not sure what to say, princess." He put his hand on her shoulder. "Brothers can be pretty mean sometimes."

"Mean? We're talking cruel here. We're talking *diabolical.*"

"I always thought you two got along pretty well."

"Eons ago, maybe, back in the Dark Ages," she said. "Now, though, I'm a modern woman, hip to male subterfuges." She screwed up her face, eyeing him suspiciously. "You're not a *spy* are you? Where's Mom?"

"You mother assured me that your feelings were not in jeopardy of permanent scarring. Me, I wasn't so sure. I'm checking in here to see if maybe a truce might be arranged . . . but I'm mostly here to tell you I care about you."

"Great, Dad. Me, I'm thinking this environment isn't big enough for both Matt and me." She pulled a printout from a stack of books. "Me, I've been investigating good prep schools. I mean, with Matt's huge, vaunted intellect, he deserves scholarships and lodging in the very best halls of academia . . . Preferably light-years distant. This would help us both grow in peace and proper nurture . . ."

Brogan glanced at the list. Earth schools. He smiled warmly. "Your concern for your brother touches me, pumpkin. I didn't know you loved him so much."

"I love him enough to know that I want him out of our sight!"

"Tell you what. We'll have a little interkingdom

diplomatic parley next week and try and settle this little scuffle. Matt's not going to any prep school. He belongs here with us, so you might as well get that out of your head."

"Rats."

"All I want from you is the promise that you'll try and not tease him. We'll figure out some other things next week and get to the heart of the matter. Meantime, how about you too just ignoring each other for a while. See how that feels."

"Sounds fine to me! I've got a life. I've got plenty of things to do besides deal with that slide rule–head. I've got friends, imaginary and otherwise. I've got school. I've got *lots!*"

"You bet. And you've got Mom and me, too."

"Yeah. Right." Sarcastically.

"What's that supposed to mean?"

"You've got important stuff to do, I know. There's not much time to deal with your retarded daughter. Maybe some kind of remedial program. I know! Maybe you can find some hot Demeter company who wants to test market their wares on *stupid* Earthlings."

"You're not stupid. You've got a lot going for you."

"Don't patronize me!"

"You see! I'm not even sure what that word means!"

"Oh. Sure."

"Hmm." He detected something familiar in her, something that irked him but also gave him pause: his own stubbornness.

"Okay. Just stopped in for a few words. Gotta

get to work." He rose off the bed. "Try and not rattle your brother's cage, okay?"

She smiled at the implied analogy. "I'll do what I can."

"I knew you would."

He kissed the top of her head, and then went off to catch the shower . . .

. . . and from there, hopefully, start work on catching a few slippery criminals.

CHAPTER

When an entire world
is devoted to a city, that city tends to sprawl.

Demeter City sprawled, and sprawled some more.

Brogan was always excited, always alarmed when he had a cruiser-eye's view of that expanse. It just went on and on . . .

. . . and on . . .

He knew the City had edges. All he had to do was to pop a map onto his viewer to see the edges. He just couldn't get them visually.

Now, as the afternoon sun winked in the glass and billowed in the polluted rivers, his police cruiser angled down to Mrax Computers, past the point of no return into another dangerous case.

"Damn!" said Haldane. "The ketchup dispenser is jammed again!"

♦ 55 ♦

"I thought you already had lunch."

"Nope. Too excited about beating your butt at racquetball. Man, I'm hungry, too!"

"Well, eat the hot dog without ketchup."

"I *like* it with ketchup."

"Look, I don't want your stomach rumbling in the middle of this investigation."

Haldane shrugged and bit into the dog.

He spit the mouthful out.

"Cold?" said Brogan.

"Worse. Constitutor bungled again. You know, you'd think in a modern galactic city, you could get yourself a modern galactic hot dog. But no . . . . Sheesh. At least in the Big Apple you can just go to the park and get yourself a nice steamed kosher dog. You know what I mean. Kraut, warmed bun, Coney Island mustard . . ."

"I thought you liked ketchup."

"It's a ketchup kind of day, okay? I go for mustard on mustard kind of days."

"Okay. Well, your stomach may rumble but at least you won't have tomato sauce all over your uniform."

"Thanks, Brogan."

"You're welcome, Haldane."

The cruiser cut through a billow of smoke. Demeter City had its clear days for sure, but just as often it was smoggy. Lots of industry down there, with not a whole lot of environmental controls. Those were slowly being implemented, thanks to help from Earth scientists and engineers. However, Demeter City was capitalism run amok, and it was hard to get money-hungry owners to plunk down the kind of cash needed to clean things up. Brogan figured that this place would have pristine air about the same time he and the police force swept crime off the streets . . . .

About the same time you could get ice-cream cones in Hell . . .

Demeter City was a damned unique place, though, so you had to cut it some slack.

It had a fascinating background.

The stars were lots closer together in this part of the Milky Way's spiral arm. It just so happened that a couple of civilizations, the Creons on planet Danae and the Tarns of planet Simter in neighboring systems, developed FTL space travel about the same time—and discovered this planet, Altor, and each other almost simultaneously. Both being easygoing races, as races go, they saw the potential in cooperation and in Altor immediately: here was a planet with no intelligent life, yet habitable, ripe for settlement. Both their civilizations had developed somehow on bleak worlds, and poverty there was the norm. On Altor, they could collaborate on prosperity and industry . . . .

Thus the Great Emigrations began, and farming of this fertile planet commenced.

Thus Demeter City, radiating around the spaceport, started its mechanical mushroom life.

Demeter City, indeed, would have remained a comparatively small city but for the fortuitous discovery that changed it . . . and the known Universe, forever.

Not far from the planet, an area of space was discovered containing a bizarre and particular kind of singularity—a stable wormhole—that was a gateway to other parts of the galaxy. Tarn and Creon ships ventured forth, discovered emerging cultures and civilizations. Trade agreements were struck. And since all shortcuts led to Demeter City, the place naturally became a galactic crossroads.

Its preexistent lassez-faire laws gave both Creon and Tarn companies opportunities for riches beyond their wildest dreams. Alas, with all the growth and opportunity that a free market provides, the money it generates inevitably creates and attracts a criminal element. In the case of Demeter City, sniffing blood, the criminal element arrived from all over the galaxy, sharpening their knives for their part of the gargantuan pie.

For a time, everything was out of control.

Then the Creons, who had the stronger police force on their home planet because of their more-violent natures, started restructuring law enforcement. Somehow, a government of sorts was emplaced, and more laws were enacted. Unfortunately, the wheels had turned too far and by then criminals—as well as eminent and bloodthirsty corporations—were entrenched into society.

Poverty conditions created more lower classes, more tough conditions; from these sorry situations arose the desperate and the greedy. Social woes and cultural confusion bred more and more problems. It was only the teamwork of Creons and Tarns, aided occasionally by companies and other races, that finally beat back the chaos to its present roar.

And into this roar had come, at the invitation of the desperate powers-such-as-they-were, Earth law enforcement instructors and personnel: including one New York cop named Patrick Brogan.

"I'm going to raise hell back at the station about this," said the other, Jack Haldane, now frantically dialing at his snack-supplier. "I mean, we troops need some energy."

"Tell you what," said Brogan. "We get down to Mrax, I'll spring for a candy bar. I'm sure they've got machines."

"Right. They'll probably have chocolate-wrapped seaweed!"

"Nah. Some of the Tarn confections are surprisingly compatible with human taste."

"Yeah! If you dig the crawling maggots out."

"Protein!"

Haldane blanched.

Brogan smiled and tapped the blinking destinator. "One Mrax Computers, coming up!"

He tapped the hopper out of computer control and dived down on manual. He was a steady, good driver—not like Haldane, who delighted in scaring the wits out of his partner with his 3-D race car driver streaks and devil-may-care turns. He descended into the blinking lights and strange patterns conservatively and well.

He set down on top of the Mrax building.

"I'm not sure if they're exactly going to be dispensing hospitality here," said Haldane, "seeing that this is a bit of an unannounced visit on our parts."

"You mean, just short of a raid."

"Yeah."

"Take it from an old hand at these kinds of—uhm—raids. Just keep a smile on your face and your hand near your gun, and you'll be surprised how cooperative the raidees can be. This uniform carries a lot of weight and intimidative weight, chum. Part of what you learn is how to use every bit you got."

"You bet. As usual, I shall watch the master. I'm, after all, the rookie in this operation."

"Right. Charm and looks and intelligence can take you only so far, Haldane. Believe one who has all three."

"And don't forget modesty!"

"One of my primary colors."

He thumbed the bubble open. The cops got out and went to the sealed entryway.

Identified themselves, demanded to speak to the proper official.

Within moments, a nervous-looking Tarn arrived at the door and opened it.

Brogan displayed his shield, and a computer reference chip.

"Name's Brogan. Demeter Police. We're investigating the murder of one of your employees."

The Tarn blinked. "Oh dear! A murder! How absolutely horrendous. We've heard of no murder. Who was the poor soul?"

"That's all we have time to tell you now," said

Haldane. He held up the search warrant. "Now we demand direct access to your computer records."

"This . . . this is most unprecedented."

"Yes, well, if you'd like, I'd be happy to show you the code that allows me to throw your butt in jail if you obstruct the swift execution of this—"

The Tarn held his hands up in horror. "Oh no! No! Please, come in. I'm really just community relations, actually. We thought perhaps you were in need of a cannoli . . . or perhaps a donut."

Haldane brightened at this possibility, but Brogan shot him a glare. "Perhaps you'd better take us to your nearest computer facility. According to code, we must do this personally . . ."

"Ahm, er . . . why yes, of course. Please step this way."

"Entering Mrax Computers," Brogan barked into his comm-unit. Of course headquarters knew very well where Brogan and Haldane were entering; Brogan just wanted to make sure that Mrax security knew they knew.

"Arm SWAT team for backup," said Haldane.

Brogan gave Haldane a "Don't you think you're going overboard?" look. Haldane shrugged.

The well-dressed community relations Tarn took them to a turboshaft. "Computer access is this way." Once inside, he punched the down button and they went for their ride. "My name is Obscue, by the way, and I'm doing what you ask under protest."

"On the record, bub," said Brogan.

"I'm really not sure why you just didn't access our computers using normal channels."

"Lots of reasons," said Haldane. "Mostly filtering. You could have a dozen doctoring systems up, and we wouldn't know it using communications lines. This way, we get to use the spot we choose, access the information we need."

"Ah, yes. Highly irregular." The Tarn shuddered with distaste. "And a violation of entrepreneurial rights. You Earthmen are Americans, no? You should be ashamed of what you're doing to your own principles."

"Sorry, but in this kind of chaos, these kinds of radical laws are necessary," said Haldane, a little too meekly for Brogan's taste.

Brogan stuck his big jaw closer to the Tarn, blasted him with some onions from lunch. "Anyway, I personally favor heading toward a police state. Would you care to be a martyr to my personal panzerblitz in that fascist direction?"

The Tarn's eyes rolled with fear. "Noooo. Noooo. But I must insist . . ."

"Insist all you like."

"I should like a token member of our security to oversee your operation."

"Just as long as my buddy's blaster gets to oversee your security officer."

Shuddering, the Tarn nodded. He used the comm to dispatch the security officer.

"Bad cop, bad cop, huh?" whispered Haldane.

Brogan shook his head. "Bad cop. Worse cop. More effective."

"Wow. You live, you learn."

"Not in this business. You learn, you *live*."

The car stopped, disgorging the passengers.

They were on the ground floor, and Brogan could see there was no doubt that this was a manufacturing facility. Machines hunkered and growled and clacked: a complex, huge array of them, with workers all about, doing their duties. Brogan could smell electricity and resistance, oil, odd alloys, alien sweat, and something oddly familiar . . .

"Pizza sauce?" said Haldane, as they were led to the computer station.

"Huh?" said Brogan.

"Yes! I smell pizza!"

"Ah yes, we take pride in the excellent New Galactic Italian cuisine," said Obscue, tartly. "If you'd been more polite, we would have offered you some initially."

An annoying, very organic noise sounded close by.

Haldane's stomach rumbling.

Brogan shot him a pained look. Haldane grabbed his abdomen, muffling the sound.

Brogan's attention had been diverted, so he had not seen the crawling figure darting out from a side aisle of machines.

He tripped.

Patrick Brogan had excellent coordination and reaction time. He tripped, rolled, came up like a practiced gymnast. And when he came up he had his gun in his hand, and it was aimed not merely at the person who had tripped him, but ready to arc toward anyone threatening him in the vicinity.

His eyes were flinty dark with business.

"Akkkkk!" squeaked their nervous guide. The Tarn dived to the floor and proceeded to quake and quiver with the exaggeration of a caricature.

"Everybody!" yelled Jack Haldane. Brogan saw with his peripheral vision that his partner had produced his own weapon, lightning-quick. Two hands gripping it: pure by-the-book procedure. "Everybody freeze!"

Brogan looked down at the person who had tripped him, and found himself staring into two highly aqua eyes set off by enough mascara to paint a picture. A bobbed nose, a full lipsticked mouth, a huge splash of blond hair and a trim, big-breasted torso above a tight red skirt. Young, emphatically human, definitely female.

"Sorry there, guy," she said, wide-eyed, as she stared into the bore of the gun. "Don't shoot!"

She had the nasal accent of a lifelong and unredeemed Queens resident, an accent that would make Henry Higgins hurry home to Eliza Doolittle.

Brogan lowered his gun. "You ought to be more careful where you crawl," he said, still cautious.

"Apologies, apologies! I just lost my ear! You ain't seen an ear lying around here, have you?" Her eyes scanned the floor. She talked around a large wad of gum.

"Your *ear!*" said Haldane.

"Yeah. What'samatter? You never saw an android lose her ear? One of our biggest problems. Ah, there it is." She reached under a machine overhang and pulled her lost appendage out, reaffixing it beneath her wealth of blond hair.

"Ah yes," said the Tarn. "This is just Betty January—our receptionologist."

"Yeah, and I answer phones, too. Ain't no way I can do that without my ear." She hobbled up onto her high heels, with a definite wobble. She smoothed her skirt, somehow releasing a waft of perfume. Even though she wasn't strictly speaking a human, Brogan couldn't help but find his heart skipping a beat at her exaggerated femininity.

"You can put your jaw back in realignment, partner," Brogan told Haldane.

"Huh? Oh—gee . . . I didn't know that androids came in your flavor, ma'am."

"Oh. Flavor? Yeah, lipstick's cherry. Wanna taste?"

"Uhm . . . ." said Haldane. "I really don't think so."

"I ain't gonna let you kiss me, guy. Wouldn't be bad though—you're kinda cute." She pulled off her bag and dragged out a lipstick holder, holding it forward. "Damned tasty, you ask me."

"Thanks anyway. Very thoughtful, though."

She shook her head. "You cops better watch out where you wave those flyswatters. You might hurt yourselves."

"Look, we've got a job to do here. Sorry about the problem ma'am." Brogan lifted an imaginary hat.

"Say. Where you goin'? I'm on my break. Can I come along and watch? Ain't every day a handsome cop comes along and falls for me!" She tittered at her joke.

"Well, it's up to them, of course, Betty . . ."

Obscue looked at the cops. "However, Betty is pretty knowledgeable about these things, and she'd be able to answer any computer questions you might have."

"Oh sure," said Betty, smiling. "I gotta know these things. I interface, like . . . . *all* the time."

"If it expedites things, of course," said Brogan.

"Come then, all of you. The necessary terminal is over here," said their guide.

The android known as Betty January needed no further invitation. She waltzed saucily after the Tarn, her shapely hips moving back and forth like a pendulum.

"Geez," said Haldane. "Looks like an old-fashioned girl."

"Let's just get on with it, Haldane," said Brogan, brushing himself off.

The Tarn led them to a computer terminal filled with an confusing array of paraphernalia.

"I believe that this is the necessary station to accomplish your work, though I bring you here under strong protest, and would remind you that all galactic forms of politeness require you to wait until the property authority—"

"We're cops from New York City, the city so nice they named it twice. Of course, we're polite," said Brogan sarcastically. "So we'll ask you to politely move your butt so we can do what we came to do. Haldane?"

"Oooh. New Yawk, New Yawk . . ." yapped the woman. "I want to wake up in the city that never sleeps!"

His partner nodded and pulled out a p-cube from his pocket.

"Primary access, buddy?" asked Brogan, looking with bewilderment at the complex array of slots and holes and buttons and what-have-you on the console.

"Pardon me?"

"How are we going to interface?" said Haldane. "I see at least five mating points."

"I *love* interfacing!" said the blonde. "I suggest you stick it there!" She pointed to the lowest slot.

"Thanks," said Haldane, glaring at the Tarn. He jammed the cube in. Instantly, the monitors changed color and graphics began to grow geometrically.

"Mating points! Such interesting language," said Betty, giggling.

As they waited for the results, Brogan turned to the android. "Receptionologist. You have a degree?"

"Oh yes. I have a great degree. Of poise, of personality, of skill. I do a little filing, I do a lot of lunch . . . And I'm a great auxiliary storage dump for transitory information. Care to look at my node array?" Beguilingly, she began to unbutton the front of her blouse.

"Uhmm . . . no, that won't be necessary," said Brogan.

"I've got a really nice pair of secondary overlay maximizers," she said.

"Yes, we can see that," said Haldane.

"And my input receptor is state-of-the-art. Mister Carbariano, he calls it the nicest little input receptor he's ever seen on the hottest little android chassis this side of Schenectady!" Betty seemed absolutely breathless and thrilled at the whole notion.

"Mister Carbariano?" said Brogan, turning to her. "And just who would that be?"

"That would be *me*, bub," said a booming male voice from behind.

Both Haldane and Brogan spun around. The voice was so bass and overridden with Hell's Kitchen threat, that Brogan had all he could do to keep from pulling out his heater.

When he got a look at the guy, he almost wished he had.

It was a Creon, the biggest Creon that Brogan had ever seen. However, the outfit was far from Creon ceremonial, distant from Creon casual, and certainly nothing like he'd seen on *this* world, anyway.

"Name's Vinnie. Vinnie Carbariano," said the guy. "Head of security here at Mrax Computers. Youse guys got yourselves a search warrant? We don't let exactly every Joe Blow onto dese premises."

Haldane handed over the warrant chit.

It was like Fay Wray in King Kong's mitt. The big guy wrinkled his nose at the writing, seeming to sniff it. Handed it back. "We got nuttin' to hide." He winked at Betty. "Hey, babe. You have a good lunch?"

"The *best*, Vinnie. A nice lube analog cacciatore."

"Dat's good. We like all our people to eat well

here at Mrax. Ya eat good, ya feel good. You feel good, you look good. You look good, Mrax Computers looks good."

The big palooka shot his cuffs, preening in his sartorial splendor.

From two-tone spit-polish shoes to sleek, slicked-back hair, the security Creon was a perfect off-the-wall rendition of mid-twentieth century mobster, straight out of Al Capp's "L'il Abner." Sleek black creased pants. Dark jacket with wide lapels on the huge shoulders and narrow waist. A striped silk tie atop a polka-dot silk shirt. He smelled of pomade and shoe polish. His eyes were mean and black.

"One of your employees was found murdered last night," said Brogan. He'd never quite encountered caricatures like this one, but he knew the cocky bluff personality. He'd dealt with it all the time in the Apple. "We'd appreciate it if you'd cooperate with our investigation."

"Oh? And who would dat be?"

"You don't keep track of who didn't come in today?" said Haldane. "You don't care about your employees." Haldane, too, was clearly having trouble reconciling himself with this refugee from "Guys and Dolls."

"Hey! Dey got personal lives. I ain't no buttin-sky." He wiggled a beckoning thumb toward Betty. She came over.

"You got a record of anyone employed by dis here company AWOL today?"

"Just a sec. I'll radiotronically interface."

Two sweet blinks. A twitch, showing a dimple. Then:

"Yes. As a matter of fact . . . Popxl Manarvan, nickname 'Haze,'" she said. "He didn't show up for work today. A call to his home produced no results. However, this has happened before . . . and Mister Manarvan showed up hours late. No particular notice was taken."

"Dat your guy?" asked Carbariano.

"That's him."

"Dead, huh?"

"As a mackerel," said Brogan

Carbariano raised a thick black eyebrow. "Manarvan. Dat name rings a bell. Sweetcakes . . . ain't that the joker, gets his nose in the numbers?"

Blink. Twitch. "Yes, as a matter of fact, Mister Manarvan regularly played our knixball lotteries," said Betty. "Not real well, I'm afraid!"

"A shame. Nice guy," said Carbariano, shrugging eloquently. "Probably stuck his nose into some floating crap game. Got some rough customers there. Maybe Haze got in a little too deep for his own health." The Creon took out a toothpick and began to work on his peculiar teeth. "See? All ya had to was to ask Betty here. Didn't have to go sticking nuttin' in our computers. What's it doing, by the way?"

"Analyzing your procedure and records . . . everything legally accessible, but you haven't tendered to the Demeter City government," said Haldane.

"Dat's okay, den. Like I say, everything about

our operation's an open book. Meantime, gentlemen . . . Can I offer you some cappuccino? Some
biscotti? You skinny guys . . . Maybe some nice
manicotti wit' some cheese. Mrax Computers likes
to show its hospitality to our folks in blue who keep
the streets safe!"

"No thanks," said Brogan. He had the worst feeling, as though he was in some absurd, abstract
nightmare. He just wanted to get through this and
get out of here for now. Think about why he was
having this reaction.

"I don't know," said Haldane, hand on abdomen.
"Smells awfully good."

Brogan tried to shoot Haldane a dirty look, but
the rookie was facing commissary-wards, sniffing
the mouth-watering aromas.

"Yeah. Dat's our new commissary. Piazza Dell
Siciliano. Ain't nothing like it on Demeter City, I
promise ya!" said Carbariano. "Hey . . . You say
you're from New York?"

"Well, Long Island in my case."

"Close enough. You do us a favor? You check our
pizza, huh? Our chefs say we got genuine New
York Pizza. You be the judge, eh?"

"Pizza. Oh dear," said Haldane. "And I don't
suppose we're talking pepperoni here?"

"Imported straight from Queens!" said Betty
with a curious proprietary glee. "You want a piece.
I'll get you one!"

With no further adieu or ado, the blond android
hurried away, heels clicking excitedly.

"Sweet kid, huh? This'll be good. We got genuine

taste testers from New York. Suddenly, why am I glad you two came?" said Carbariano.

Brogan tried to get back to business. "I've got a little problem, Mister Carbariano, and I'm not going to mince words here. Manarvan was found in a couple of concrete gravity boots, sailing for the stars. Now, back in the New York I believe the tradition was the East River, but the disposal system looks extremely familiar. I'm having a little trouble here. . . . Italian food, ditzy receptionist android . . . and you're a Creon, for God's sake. Why have you got yourself decked out like cheap Dago muscle?"

A flicker of anger moved over the big face. Violence, lightning, thunder in those dark eyes. "You want I should call you a Mick, Brogan? We try to be politically correct here." He straightened his tie, slightly self-consciously.

"Call me what you like. Just explain to me what's going on here?"

"I don't know what you're talking about, but if it ain't got nothing to do with your investigation, then I can't help you," said Carbariano. "Way I see it, my job is to keep this place secure. That's why dey call me security head. This ain't no kind of safe world. Thusly, youse guys are my buds. 'Cause that's *your* job . . . keepin' this place safe, too. Keepin' this company safe, 'cause we pay *plenty* of taxes."

"Who do you report to, Mister Carbariano?" asked Brogan.

"I report to Da Boss."

"And who would that would be?"

"That would be Mister Da Chancio."

"And would it be possible to speak to Mister Da Chancio?"

"He's weekending on the Eden PowerSki WinterSport slopes."

"How slippery of him. Could you have him give the department a call when he gets back—at his earliest possible convenience, of course."

"Natch! No prob. How's that little thing doin' there?" The big guy peered down at the graphics doing elaborate Euclidean widdershins upon the screen. "Busy little bastard, isn't he?"

Betty January hurried back, holding a platter dominated by two gigantic wedges of what was unmistakably pepperoni pizza. The aroma was equally unique and more than tempting.

"Hey there, Officer Brogan. I brought you a piece too," she said, somehow looking simultaneously sexy and innocent.

Haldane helped himself shamelessly to the pizza. He stuck into his mouth and bit off a huge piece. The delight in his eyes was pure and perfect. He gestured down to the proffered pizza as though it were the Holy Grail itself. "Tastes just like Sal's Original. Maybe even better!" Muffled through a mouthful.

"Try it!"

Brogan felt his taste buds kicking him in the rear end, but he just couldn't do it. "Thanks, but no thanks."

"Officer Haldane gets two, then!" said the public relations officer.

"On da house!" proclaimed Carbariano.

Grimacing, Brogan turned around toward the screen.

CIRCUIT COMPLETE. DATA STORED.

"You'd better get a doggy bag, then. We're finished." He popped the cube out, pocketed it.

"I'll just go and get you a box," said the public relations officer. "Perhaps, when you finish, you can radio back a quote for our kitchen."

"I'll give you a quote right now. 'Wow.' You guys deliver?"

"Haldane!"

"Sorry."

"Come back any time, guys!" said Betty January cheerfully.

"Yeah," said big Carbariano, pulling out a cigar the size of a torpedo. He bit off the end and spit it out. A little robot shaped like a spittoon came out of nowhere and intercepted the fallen piece. A laser beam erupted from the little robot, lighting the security chief's smoke. "Be our guest."

The unctuous public relations man returned forthwith with a perfectly sized cardboard box. The extra piece, along with the bit that Haldane had not eaten, were placed within, and the police were politely shown to the door.

Brogan looked behind him as they walked toward the exit.

Vinnie Carbariano and Betty January stood like Monster and Maiden, waving farewell in perfectly synchronous, perfectly bizarre motion.

"Bye!"

"Yeah. Bye-bye, good friends!"

Brogan looked over at a monitor that was just flashing off.

For the life at him, he thought he'd seen a picture of someone far more upsetting, waving goodbye as well.

CHAPTER

"**Where your ass is now**," said the troll, "is the Crack of Doom."

"Oh yeah?" Matt Brogan twisted hard on the joystick, tapping in a surprise spell on the keyboard at the same time. Happily, the ingenious spell (created by ingenious Matt, brilliantly improvising on the basic rules set up by the sim) raced through the puzzle-maze, dissolving the troll's flux-defense spell.

Matt's computer-generated holographic sword whacked through the troll. Ectoplasmic blood—in radical strains of purple and crimson—washed down onto the desk.

"Urrghhh!" gurgled the troll, falling (in two graphic pieces, displaying trollish viscera) onto the greensward. Victorious Matt was provided a moment to regard the messy results before the dumb-magic creature dissolved, leaving the path to the Treasure Tree open.

Cautiously (for who knew what other perils might spring up in the intervening space?) Matt went to the tree. (Or rather, the holographic VirtReal Holo-Panoply showed the tree approaching, and Matt had the Hero's-Eye View of his sword, shiny and bloody, advancing before him).

He called forth the key he had discovered in the Stagnant Caves—and then he called forth the best of the algorithm spells he'd developed.

Lubricated by the spell, the key went into the lock effortlessly. The wooden door opened.

Gold coins, emeralds, rubies, diamonds, and other items of incalculable worth and magnificent splendor (twinkly and gleaming stylistically with an artist's touch) poured out of the Treasure Tree below the sword.

A sonorous voice intoned.

"Congratulations, young knight. You have successfully completed this level of the sim. Please fill out the questionnaire concerning your opinion at your leisure, and return, utilizing the most convenient method."

Matt turned the computer off and grinned.

Pixie dust glittered in the air, and then was gone.

Well, it was an okay sim, he supposed. The Spell Originating was the innovative aspect—teaching different kinds of logic of formula methods, and would be good for educational purposes.

What Matt liked most was the blood and guts.

A small smile grew on his face . . . blood and guts . . . nasty monsters . . . and those Thorny Banshees were some of the most horrific, shrieking holo-effects he'd ever seen in a sim.

Something like that would scare the bejesus out of his little sister!

He turned the computer back on, went quickly into the machine language, tweaked this and that with rapid taps of the keyboard.

A few minutes later, he emerged from his twiddlings, and then hit the initiation segment of the sim program.

A new title flashed into the air:

FUZZY WARM CRYSTAL BUNNY
RABBIT TREASURE HUNT!

Glowing with flowers. Twinkling with a hoppy, smiling bunny, beckoning innocent pleasure seekers.

Heh heh heh!

He turned the computer back off.

Yes. Maybe his parents were right. Maybe he *should* allow dear, sweet Liz to play this new game with him. She was such a forlorn and left-out little girl, and surely bunny rabbits would cheer her up.

Anyway, it would be a good joke.

His parents would come down on him—but it was only make-believe. A puff of a few lights. Boo!

Perhaps dear sis wouldn't be so jealous anymore then—and she would watch where she stuck her big nose!

He looked at his watch.

Four-fifty-five. Almost time for "All My Aliens," one of their favorite programs. They even watched it together sometimes.

He'd make his "peace offering" suggestion while they were watching the show.

It wasn't like she'd have a heart attack or anything. She just had to learn not to always want to poke that big nose of hers into guy stuff. He'd probably get lectured by Mom or Dad—but hey, that was their job.

And as Big Brother, it was his job to keep Little Sister in line.

Matt Brogan nodded happily to himself as he left. And all this grand fun was going to be for *free!*

After the light was switched off and the door closed, the teenager's room stayed still and dark for several moments.

Then a light clicked on from the cube slot into which the new program had been stuck.

The casing of the CPU bubbled and shifted, and extended a tentative strand of metal, like a pseudopod from an amoeba.

CHAPTER

Podly leaned back in
his seat, clutching his mug of green, aromatic
mucca-stim as though it were his absolute best
friend in the entire known Universe.

He regarded Brogan and Haldane with a
thoughtful, deep gaze.

"You two did good. Real good."

Brogan had just debriefed him, and he did so still
not quite believing his experience back at Mrax.

"Thanks. I'm a bit bemused," said Brogan.

"Me too. A strange place." Haldane cupped a burp
with his hand and patted his stomach happily.

"Of course you are. And well you should be."
Podly tapped his monitor, upon which photos and
details of the dead informants were displayed.
"There have been a few complications tossed into
the stew."

"Something that could explain things?" said Brogan.

"Not quite. We were hoping that maybe you might be the judge of that." He hit an intercom. "Castle? Do you have your report yet?"

"Just a sec, sir," chirped the woman brightly. "I'm just printing out now."

"Don't bother. Just route the stuff to my info display."

"Yes sir. Won't be but a twitch of the keyboard."

"Snap it up, Castle. I've just been debriefing Haldane and Brogan and we've got quite the situation . . . "

"Haldane and Brogan without their briefs? Must be quite the sight."

"No time for snappy comebacks, Castle," said the gruff Creon. "Barely time for quick appearances!"

"Yes sir. It's up, sir! And so will I be, just as soon as these obedient legs get me there."

Castle turned off the comm, and leaned forward. "You Earthers. I don't know why I get stuck with the likes of you. Gab gab gab." Podly shook his big head sorrowfully. "Almost as bad as Creons!" He tried to summon the info by tapping on his screen controls, grumping as he searched for the promised material.

Brogan sipped at his coffee, feeling trepidation fidget. Podly had the air of someone who wanted to go late night with this. Brogan wanted to file his report, get an early start for home and start fresh next week. Whatever was happening could keep, in his humble opinion.

He wasn't real happy with the way his kids were relating. It was these damned late shifts, he was sure of it; he really should be spending more time with them, especially during this formative stage. Cripes, with him not around much, who knew what kind of father figure they'd fixate on in the middle of alien civilizations. Talk about alienated teenagers!

As for Haldane, he looked as though he could use a good Galacta Seltzer.

Cursing, Podly stabbed at the comm.

"Castle! Castle, where the bloody hell is—"

"I'm here, sir," said the officer, arriving pell mell, looking a little more in disarray than was her usual wont.

"I can't get your damned files up, Castle!" said Podly.

Castle stepped forward blithely. She somehow insinuated herself between hulking Podly and diminutive keyboard. Pursing lips, she examined the keyboard, touched the sensa-screen with a finger, then hit a key.

Information unfolded like an ugly mutant flower.

"There you are, sir," she said brightly. "Perhaps a little refresher course in CompMethodology."

Podly waved her away gruffly. "I don't want to hear it, Castle. Just put it up on the big screen and hit the vu-dampers and privacy shield. I don't want the whole station knowing our business here."

"Yes sir."

Dampers came up, shield came down. For all

practical purposes, they were in their own sound-proof room. Podly liked this arrangement. Not only could he provide himself instant privacy—but he could spring out of that privacy equally instantly, to make sure his people were hard at their work and not lollygagging about.

Castle switched the info to the main screen.

"This is your stuff, Jane," said Podly, looking a little less arrogant and bluff—honestly troubled now as he surveyed the material. "Please present it."

Castle turned to the officers, and suddenly she wasn't the chipper, clever English girl anymore. She was the Englishwoman in the middle of World War II, talking about Nazi troop movements. "Right. I burned a lot of computer circuitry on this one. I got all the available information here and had a top priority jump-pulse requisitioned through the 'hole from Earth, so we have all the necessary corporate and criminal records from back there.

"Cost and Gnostra is a corporation formed under Demeter law. However, it has a parent corporation back on Earth, and it shares two directors. That corporation back home is Alfonso Securities. The two directors are Bennet Tenaglia and Jack Loren. Ring any bells, Brogan?"

Brogan though for a moment. Then the answer came up. "Tenaglia and Loren. Those names . . . yeah, I helped put away two guys involved in a huge drug operation and murder named Tenaglia and Loren. They were older guys, though, and they got cooled for good."

"They were a part of that final closedown of organized crime, right?"

"Yeah. Project Crackdown. Twenty years in the making with a cast of thousands. I was involved, sure, but only in one facet."

"You're right. These aren't the mobsters you helped put away." Castle paused. "They're the sons. And get this. They have a little organization. A computer BBS, a magazine, a publishing company. They call themselves the Mothers' and Fathers' Italian Association. An acronym, of course, for Mafia."

"Mafia," said Podly. "Even I've heard about the Mafia, from my studies of Earth police history. A form of organized crime started in Sicily and spread to the United States."

"They can *do* that?" said Brogan.

"They're all highly educated and make plenty of money from other corporations . . . mostly sci-tech. It's a hobby and quite in the open. They claim to be historians—cultural preservers. They even pay taxes. All very aboveboard."

"Sci-tech, you say . . ." said Brogan. "That explains why they'd start a computer company on Demeter City. And maybe even the preoccupation with twentieth-century motifs. The organized crime I dealt with were just criminals . . . they didn't look like covers of pulp magazines."

"And everything they do seems aboveboard as well, on the record," said Castle. "I ran the 'cube you brought back. There's nothing on it that doesn't match with the records of the company presented to public authority or that is in any way approaching illegality or even hints of illicit activity. They make computer parts, period. If they want to dress funny and serve Italian food in their commissary, there's certainly nothing illegal about that, right?"

"What about four dead informants, oodles of crime in traditional Mob fashion, and a smell very distinctly of rat." Haldane cocked a thumb toward his partner. "To say nothing of Brogan's gut."

"Nothing that links Mrax or Cost and Gnostra or anyone we're investigating. Our hands are tied here. We've found nothing we can act upon legally."

"Sci-tech," said Brogan, a little niggling something going on in the back of his head. "Can you be more specific?"

"The whole array. Energy companies. Space drive companies . . . but the one you might find interesting, Brogan, is the gen-tech company. Drexler Subsidiaries."

"I thought that went out of business." A stab of alarm shot up Brogan's spine.

"Apparently it was bought and brought back into business," said Castle, tapping a line of print. "And when you look through all the business prestidigitation, you can see that these two men . . . They're the sons of a complex weave of international organized crime on Earth."

"Would someone care to turn on the wind machine and get my head out this fog?" said Podly. "Am I supposed to see something?"

Brogan shook his head. "I didn't realize that it

would go back that deeply." He shook his head as though to clear it. "Sorry, Chief. I can see what Jane's getting at. One of the mobsters I personally brought down was the owner of Drexler. He was also linked with organized crime in a very real way—And he was *also* a former college chum. I guess that just about puts it into a nutshell."

Podly squinted at the screen. "That would be Dominick Monteleone."

"That's right, sir."

"But it says here he's deceased."

Brogan swallowed. "Yeah. I can verify that. I shot him myself."

Haldane looked quickly at his partner. "Damn. That must have been rough."

"Yeah. It wasn't easy. Of course, the guy had become a murderer and extortionist and a racketeer of incredible proportions, and he had to be stopped."

"But he used to be your friend."

"Officers," said Podly, "this isn't group therapy. If this Monteleone character is dead, he's dead. What concerns me right now is the significance of this company that Tenaglia and Leone felt it worth buying. If this is a criminal operation, what's the use of a gen-tech company? And by gen-tech, I assume you mean genetic engineering. Recombinant DNA. Stuff of that ilk."

"If you'll read the fine print there, Chief Podly, you'll see something more."

Podly leaned, squinted. "Nun technology? Faith! What's that?"

"Nanotechnology," said Brogan. "That was Monteleone's obsession, even back at Columbia. I don't think it ever really worked out for him the way he thought it might."

"Aren't those the little submicrobe machines? Like little robots you can inject in your bloodstream to eat up cancers or repair damaged cells."

"Yes. Dominick had some wild ideas about the potential for nanotechnology back in college. Family was involved in organized crime and he got sucked back into the Business. Next time I met up with him, he was up to his eyebrows in it."

"So you don't know exactly what he was doing with the Drexler Subsidiaries he started up," asked Castle.

"Nope. It's a long story, but basically he tried to suck me into his shenanigans. It didn't work. And he ended up dead as a part of the whole operation—and I gotta tell you, the very thought of that kind of organized crime rearing its ugly head again—on Demeter City yet—just makes my blood run cold."

"We can't chance letting that happen," said Podly. "Not if it's got even a toehold. We got enough problems with criminals here on our own turf, without infamous syndicates sprouting." He pounded on his desk. "We're going to get to the bottom of this. You hear me?" He swung his big eyes toward Castle. "Anything else on that screen there I'm not getting?"

"Well, just a lot of equipment shipped from Earth. Start-up. Nothing that didn't pass . . ."

"Cripes, with the rotten security we've got on Demeter, who knows what they got in here." He folded his arms over his chest. "There's only one thing to be done . . ."

Haldane rolled his eyes.

"What gives me the idea it has something to do with me."

"Yes, it involves all of you. You're going back to Mrax Computers. Tonight. Late."

Brogan nodded grimly. "If we can get to the bottom of this, it will be worth it. What's the plan?"

"In that cube I gave you," said Castle, "there wasn't simply a probe. There was a secret program. We need only to initiate it via a communications line, utilizing pass-phrases we extracted in the cube. The program will permit us entrance, and all mechanical operations will consider us to be workers—indeed, obey our instructions."

"Once there," Podly continued, "you will investigate the facilities thoroughly. And Castle will personally inspect the computer operations, installing other programs that will allow us to keep tabs on the comings and goings of the people under investigation."

Brogan nodded. "Okay, Chief. We know the way there."

"Castle's got the details. You'll be moving out at 2200 hours. In the meantime, take your dinner break and go over your battle plan."

They assented to the plan and the privacy shields were lifted.

Officer Orrinn, a Creon with a batch of hair that

looked like long, frizzy peach fuzz, was waiting outside.

"Lieutenant Brogan, sir. Your wife called. Bit of a slight domestic crisis. Something to do with a sim program, a traumatized daughter . . . and a son in convulsions of laughter."

"Thanks, Orrinn," said Brogan.

"Wanna talk about it, guy?" said Haldane.

"Yeah," said Brogan. "Over a pizza and a beer. But give me a rain check. And make that pizza frozen, of the awful Demeter kind, huh? I'm not real big on the pure New York Mediterranean stuff these days."

CHAPTER

"Gin!"

The alien laid down his hand.

Its tentacles wiggled with delight.

Across, on the other side of the desk, Dominick Monteleone tallied up his points, tabulating them on a pad of paper with an old-fashioned number-two pencil.

"That puts you over a hundred, *mi amico*."

"Which means I win?" said Licknose.

"Absolutely. Very well played." Dominick Monteleone picked up a bottle of wine and filled his glass. Streams of smoke twined up from his cigarette. The good scents of cheese and fresh baked bread filled the penthouse with his favorite ambience. He felt deliciously comfortable. . . .

The fact that he had just lost the game of gin rummy meant nothing much. In fact, he had engineered the loss, to give his associate a feeling of accomplishment, victory, and belonging.

Victory was always forged by affiliation, alliance.

Little favors bred loyalty.

At least among humans. True, Licknose wasn't a human. However, as far as Monteleone could tell from his experience so far with extraterrestrials, the wisdom of his Mediterranean forbears still held true.

People (read carbon-based sentient life-forms) *needed* things. You help them get what they need, they help you get what you need. Now if *your* needs are a little grandiose . . . well so be it. You just give lots of people what they need. And if your needs are for riches and power and, ultimately, *control*—Well, those, then, are your needs.

Monteleone had always dreamed of distant planets, of future vistas. This was one part of the reason for his fascination with the subject areas of his expertise. From the smallest one forged the largest . . . Molecules, atoms . . . subatomic material formed the bridges that could span the stars. The key to the macro was in the micro . . . .

Principles his *compaisanos* had taught him.

Lessons learned from the deep vault of riches of his family.

He gazed thoughtfully out at the cityscape, the alien cupolas and vaulting bridges, the twisted turrets and the mangled minarets. All the visionaries of Earth's past, in their artistic idylls into the future, could never have realized just how much this bizarre city would be so like Earth's city . . .

And how little . . .

The phone rang.

It wasn't a comm-unit, it was a phone. Big, black, circa 1930s Earth, blending in perfectly with the design of the huge penthouse office.

Monteleone picked it up. "Yes?"

"Boss," said a voice.

"Ah. Mister Carbariano. *Mi goombah.* I've been expecting your call."

He watched passively as the alien took a few moments to do an odd wiggly Dance of Celebration, thanking his squirmy gods for this most-lauded victory at cards. How delightful!

"They're gone," said Carbariano in his thick accent. "Dey got nuttin'."

"Hmmm. I wonder about that. These *poliziotto* are not stupid."

"What's dere to get? This gear ain't even connected to the real lot."

"Perhaps. But knowing Patrick Brogan, I'd say he's got experts working with him. Brogan's smart, and Brogan's always had smart backup. He knows what he does best . . . Let me just have a look."

Monteleone tapped a button on the overhang of his desk. A large section of teak rolled back and a computer console emerged. It looked like something from a Jules Verne novel. Monteleone had had it designed precisely to suit his ornate tastes in that direction. The monitor blossomed. Monteleone played with the keys, and diagnostics commenced.

"I did observe them on the viewers," said

Monteleone, as he waited for the whizzing graphics to pop up with their tale. "Brogan looks fit, if a little dour, these days. And he seems to have an able partner."

"Yeah. Guy by da name of Haldane. Liked your pizza recipe."

"Ah. Good taste, then. Glad to hear it."

The shifting colors on the monitor jelled.

"Boss, I got one question?"

"Yes, Mister B?"

"When do I get ta waste 'em?"

"Patience, patience, Mister B. Simple oblivion is too good for my old friend Patrick Brogan. I'm looking at the diagnostic right now. Their scan seems to have been quite thorough. As you say, they obtained nothing revealing our true purposes here, nor even any of our . . . ah, traditional family operations." As he said it, he savored the words. Family. Was there ever a more meaningful, more rich concept?

"I told ya, Boss!"

"However, what you seemed to have missed, Mister Carbariano, is the fact that another program was unleashed that appears to be hiding most cleverly. If I had not been looking for it, I certainly would not have found it. From a quick glance, it looks as though it paves the way for a successful return—through your security, and from all signs, directly to exactly what they are seeking. With Brogan's style, I'd say that we can expect them tonight."

"Huh? No way. Not now . . . You tell me what they did, I'll fix it. I'm a good security man."

"You are indeed, Mister B. No aspersions cast. However, take no extra security precautions per se . . ."

"Ya mean you're just gonna let them breeze right on in here, Boss? What, are you nuts?"

"Some people might think so. . . . Psychiatrists, perhaps. Psychologists. However, I merely consider my present psychology to be—fundamentally different. No, Mister B. We're going to allow them to enter, and then close the door tight on them. We'll have some interesting diversion planned. I assume you're free tonight?"

"What? 'Course I am. That's my job. I'm here for you. I'll just call up and shoosh away all the dames."

"Good for you. I assure you, there will be amusement provided. I'll meet you there for preparations in—shall we say, an hour. I don't think our guests will be arriving *that* soon."

"I'm here now. I'll just keep an eye out."

"Of course you will, Mister B. We'll see you then."

"Ciao."

Monteleone rang off and looked over at his alien ally finishing up the last movements of his peculiar and somewhat oily dance.

"Mister Licknose. If I may have your attention for a moment. I'm going to be needing your services . . . your machines . . . and your expertise in this matter."

The alien settled down. Oozed back into its chair, leaning over, its translator rippling excitedly. "I will be of service!"

"I think we'll be doing a little bit of Real Virtuality this evening. It will be of much education and use . . . to us both . . . And will eliminate some obstacles in our path to the control of Demeter City in the process."

The tentacles and flesh/hair mat rippled with approval. The creature loosened its anticipatory odors, somewhat acrid to Monteleone's sense, but welcome nonetheless.

Yes, Demeter City was a launching point to a fabulous future, beyond dreams, beyond dazzling fulfillment. . . .

And it was a finishing point to a long-planned vengeance.

CHAPTER

Night on Demeter City.

Neon and freon.

Sparklings and rivers of welcoming light.

Lakes and holes of alien darkness.

There was a beauty here, thought Lieutenant Patrick Brogan, as he grimly guided his hopper down toward this evening's destiny. A painful beauty, and a frightening ugliness.

Amid the fumes and the jarring architecture, a message seemed writ large to him in fevered lettering:

THIS IS NOT YOUR HOME.

And yet, Demeter City was the future. The future not just for sentient races from unimaginable distances, but the future of the human race.

Humans could not turn their backs on the stars and all they meant . . . That's why people like Brogan had to go and stake their claims. Move their furniture here, teach, learn . . . acclimate, grow.

Damned hard job, though.

Especially if, all in all, you'd rather be back plunged in your warm crystal-stream tub, sudsing it up with your wife, while your two rambunctious kids were safely locked away in slumber.

Instead of out here, heading into sure and certain danger.

"Glad to have company, Castle," said Haldane. "I'm feeling waves of cold from Mr. Grim here. He doesn't seem to be very talkative this evening I'm afraid."

"I'm not sure if I would be, Haldane. Not with the kind of load that must be on his mind now."

"Yeah, sorry. Ghosts of the past and all that. I guess I'm not being real sensitive. Maybe I miss the old jocular, sardonic Brogan and I'm just expressing my own grief in a safety valve kind of mode."

"Can it, Haldane," said Brogan, eyes steady on the bit of turf he'd picked out for landing. It was a perch they'd used before: a dank but wide alley between two monolithic buildings connected by a flying buttress. Bums used to hang out or sleep here—until cops began favoring it for a parking space. Generally, street folks could see or hear a hopper roaring down from a long distance. Brogan and Haldane took to their feet from time to time to keep the cutpurses on their toes in this troubled area. Since it was only a few blocks to the entrance of Mrax Computers, it was a convenient space. "I'll talk about it when I feel this case warrants it."

He swallowed back anger. But it wasn't anger at Haldane. It was the anger and self-hatred that he still stored in the deepest part of his being. . . .

He'd killed his best friend, his roommate at college. Worse, he'd seen the path . . . no, the chasm yawning before Dominick. He should have done *something* to help him. Dominick, in different ways, had almost begged him . . . short of actually verbalizing his terror at the forces that were buffeting him. Now, as he entered a company that had sinister ties to the sorry and frightening part of his past, deep and ambivalent emotions roiled inside of him.

The hell of it was that, ultimately, one of the reasons he had left Earth was to get away from those feelings—feelings that dripped from the pretty facades of Little Italy. Feelings that he saw in every dark-eyed, olive-skinned face in a city full of them. Nick . . . Oh Nick.

"Haldane, please. Give it a rest," said Castle as the cruiser neatly settled into its place, blowing up newspaper sheets and other flotsam. "Cops aren't partnered up just for the sake of verbal comfort. Just think how precious little wit you provide for Brogan. Why . . . I bet it's just about half-regulation."

"Ha ha ha. Okay, sorry. I'm just concerned that's all," said Haldane. "We're okay, partner. No hard feelings despite my brutish, intrusive ways." He made a face at Castle. "See. I've a vocabulary, too."

"Forget about it, Haldane," said Brogan. "I'm the one who should apologize. I'm the one who's a bit snappish. Now let's get our gear together and get this baby on the road. Sooner we get in, the sooner we get out, and the happier I'll be."

Quickly, they hopped to it, hoisting their packs atop their backs, and adjusting their black null-suits and pulling up their masks. *No blues tonight*, thought Brogan. No, tonight was mission commando night. This was supralegal stuff . . . But ultimately, he knew that Podly had made the right call.

It was a call that he would have made himself.

After securing their car, they silently and quickly made their way to Mrax, the others leading Castle, who didn't know the streets as well as they. Brogan breathed in the damp and odd air, grateful for the silence of the streets now, the exercise that oddly cleared his head. It was like a meditation, the cadence of his steps comforting and focusing him. *You're a cop, Brogan. You're a cop,* they seemed to say. And a damned good one, too, he added to himself. The reminder kicked him out of his feelings. He had a job to do. Two decades plus of police work and training kicked in, and he gladly surrendered the reins of control.

At the security checkpoint, they stopped.

"That's it?"

"We haven't been to this one, but the one we used today is totally sealed at night."

Haldane pulled out a pocket radio, spoke into it. "Entrance attained. We're going in now."

"Roger," said Podly. "Backup will be hovering. You got trouble, just call. We'll come and blast you out."

Haldane clicked off. "Comforting thought. But I seriously doubt if any radio signal—special secret police band or not—is going to be getting past those walls."

"Who's to tell . . ." said Jane. "We'll just have to wait and see." She was into professional mode now, Brogan could see, and he felt comforted by her presence. Jane Castle was young, but she was accomplished. She'd whizzed through her schooling in her teens, an ace at computers. However, her heart was in the many fascinating aspects of lawkeeping. Her family was among the first to travel to Demeter City, right after she'd graduated from Police Academy. She was a natural to be among the first to work side by side with Demeter police. Because of her brilliance with computers and tactical matters, she more often worked from behind her desk than not—which was why actually getting out on a job like this, into the thick of things as it were, clearly pleased her. Brogan was just damned glad to have her along for the ride. They wouldn't be this far without her, and they wouldn't be able to get any farther, that was sure.

Haldane clearly had a little bit of a problem with her, though. "Wait and see, huh. Oh, great planning, Castle."

Haldane's trouble was simple. He had the hots for

her, and all that testosterone flowing into him wasn't getting any response from her estrogen. Result: agitation and frustration on the guy's part.

Time to shut this down.

"Haldane," said Brogan. "Tell you what. You play nice, we'll get you a pizza in there. Okay?"

"When the moon hits your eye like a big pizza pie, Haldane," said Castle tartly.

"That's amore. We'll at least my affections for the stuff tend to get returned," said Haldane. "At least pizza is warm."

"Work starts now, Haldane," said Brogan.

"Okay, okay. Cripes, two date nights . . . Shot! I'll survive though. The yap is closed."

They approached the security monitor station. Jane Castle produced three cards. One of these she slotted into the technology.

"Ah. Greetings!" said a voice. "You are expected. Please take advantage of our commissary," said a voice.

Force screens buzzed off. Door opened. The way was opened up to them.

"Just in case." She slotted the other two, then hit a button. All three were returned. "Just in case, this is your ID card for this little nocturnal excursion." She handed them the plastic.

"That's it?" said Brogan.

"No retinal patterns checked, no DNA sampled?"

"Oh, usually, of course. My program, though, circumvents all that."

"And we can just waltz on in, just like that?" said Haldane.

"Whistling the 'Blue Danube,' if you like," said Castle. "Nonetheless, it would behoove us to have our firearms ready and be on our guard. We're technically trespassers now. Legally, we're a bit at sea. Podly blows hard about being backup, but actually his hands are rather tied."

"That's okay. This has got to be done. Come on," said Brogan.

They walked through the open doors, and down a half-lit corridor, toward the murmur of machines, firearms unstrapped with hands close to them.

Something scurried past them. Haldane whipped his gun out, trained. Brogan stopped him. "Just a cleaning robot, guy. Settle down."

"Yeah. Right. Sorry, Brogan." His eyes calmed, and Brogan saw the familiar professionalism finally start to cover his gestures, expressions, movements.

"That's okay."

They led Castle out into the main portion of the factory, among the glowing, working machines, aglitter with purpose and industry. The occasional small maintenance robot rolled along among them—but no living creatures could be spotted, as Castle had predicted.

So far so good.

The question remained now:

"All right," said Haldane. "We're here. Where to next, Castle?"

"Perhaps you could guide me to that main workstation. There's an area of this system which was in shadow on the schematic provided."

"We're not being observed," said Haldane.

"That's all taken care of," said Castle. "We certainly are, but it's all automatic, and we're accepted as normally being here by the security computers."

"Right. Why are my hackles still up?"

"Cool it, right? Every sensor in here reads us as innocent as you are of experience with women, Haldane."

"Hey, wait a minute . . . I've had plenty of women!"

"Please, please. Castle, you know, if you didn't bait him . . ."

"Sorry. He's just so cute when he gets red. No time for this anyway," said the woman. "As I was saying, there's a shadowy area I need to check out myself. Please show me where that main workstation is."

"Right. It's over here."

They led her there. She unwrapped her bag of goodies and proceeded to slip cubes into slots. Then she brought out a drill.

"Say, I hope you'll be careful with that. We don't want to raise any alarms," said Brogan as he observed.

"I know what I'm doing, Brogan."

She hit the trigger.

BRRRRRRAAPPPPPPPP!

The drill bit into the metal and plastic.

Bits flew everywhere.

"Sheesh! A little extreme, don't you think?" said Haldane, hands over his ears.

"Everything's under control." Castle noisily commenced to drag stuff out of the computer. It banged onto the floor. "I've programmed the security system to accept this as normal as the flush of toilet."

"It's making *me* nervous, that's for sure."

"Yes, well, you just have no faith, Haldane." She tweaked and twitched, coaxing out a modular board. "I thought so! Let me just plug this little guy in . . . like so . . . and then nudge it into obedience." She banged it with the handle of the drill. Hard.

"The wonders of high tech!" said Haldane.

"Yes, well, scoff if you like," retorted Castle. "However, take a look."

Brogan looked. Indeed, the graphics display had changed on the monitors. Indecipherable 3-D connecting spheres and cubes and cylinders looked like some madman's Tinkertoy set.

"That's supposed to make sense?" said Brogan.

"It makes sense to me," said Castle, beaming. "And it's rather just as I thought." She pointed a slender finger. "Have a gander, gentlemen."

Her fingernail was clicking upon some kind of trapezoid arrangement.

"Looks like Euclid's undershorts to me," said Haldane, scratching his head.

"That, esteemed colleagues, is an entirely different section of computer operations . . . . A whole segment here, in this building, which my probe, that you so kindly brought here, was unable to penetrate."

"Good. Can you get into it from here?"

"I'm going to give that a go right now."

Her fingers played a tap dance over the keys.

She examined the results.

"In a word, no."

"Oh. So what's the call then?"

"I'm afraid that this arrangement is organized in such a way as to necessitate a visit into the"— she called up a schematic of the floor arrangement of the facilities—"subbasement."

"And how is that possible?" said Brogan.

"No turbolift. Stairs. Over . . ." A pointing finger arose, wavered. Straightened authoritatively. "There. Yes, that way, down through that corridor, take a left, about thirty more meters. Third door to the left."

"Sounds like a reasonable trek. We going to put that stuff back together?" said Brogan.

"Yes, on the way back. I'm strongly suspecting that it's not going to really make any difference."

"Why's that?" said Haldane.

"If they've taken precautions to separate a portion of a computer to prevent penetration of a sophisticated program like mine . . . I'm positive they must be hiding something. This could be the key to the operations that we want. That's why we're here."

"Maybe some of us are here for more of that pizza," said Haldane. "But you know, this *does* sound pretty damned important. Good work, Castle."

She reorganized her kit, straightened her null-suit, and attended to its controls. "As my programs were only effective through the main portion of the computer, I can't say for sure what they'll do for security in the subbasement. My best guess for the reading is that the security stuff is all of a piece. However, we should take every precaution."

"You bet," said Brogan. He opened the Velcro pocket of his own suit, thumbed up the controls. Null-suits created an electro-optical field around their wearers. It helped them blend in with their surroundings, night or day—and it absorbed detection beams.

"Following suit!" said Haldane, who made the adjustment.

Then they moved out, Brogan in the lead.

Quietly, they moved down the corridor sided by the strange components of this odd alien computer system. Barely audible whisperings moved along the hallways. Synthetic songs, neuronic echoes, answered in discordant mechanical harmonies. The place smelled less like an Italian restaurant now, more like an alien factory, with the odd astringencies and sweetnesses in the air.

The night lighting was like some German expressionist silent film.

So it was startling to have a blast of color and movement emerge in front of them.

It was even more startling to realize who that movement belonged to.

Jane Castle's immediate reaction was to bang against the wall, producing her gun and establishing a regulation preparatory stance.

"Hold it, Castle," said Brogan. "Not necessarily dangerous."

The figure was carrying an armful of files. Startled by the whispering, she turned to see who it was—and ran into a corner abutment. Her files spewed.

"Oh rats!" she said.

"A danger only to herself," said Haldane.

It was Betty January, in all her blond, gum-popping glory.

"Oh hi, you guys!" she said, "Whatcha doin' back here?"

"We forgot to do something," said Haldane. "Yeah. And I was hoping to pick up a pizza, too."

She blinked her huge eyelashes.

"Well, you could have just *called*. That's okay, it's good to see ya again. I'm workin' late on a project . . ." She glanced with confusion at the gun-pointing Castle. "Who's your funny friend?"

"Oh, that's Jane. She's a cop too, but she's a nervous cop. Jane, this is Betty January," said Brogan, in a forced tone to signal significance to his colleague. "Betty's an android. She works here, and she's been a great deal of help to us."

"Ah . . . right. Nice to meet you, Betty!" She couldn't help but stare at the android's exaggerated and dated feminine characteristics.

Betty was all smiles. "Pleased to meet *you!*" Betty reached out and shook Castle's hand. Jane looked at Brogan with bafflement.

"Betty's a cheerful soul and a credit to this establishment!" said Brogan.

"You better believe *that*'s true."

"We better help you with these files, huh?" said

Haldane, kneeling down and starting to pick up the folders.

"That's so *kind* of you. It's my own fault, really. You're probably asking yourself, what's a gorgeous ball of fun like me doing working on a Saturday night? Well, I already was out on the town and just wasn't having *any* fun. And we androids don't need sleep . . . We just get a little downtime each night, you know, to rest the circuits. So I came in to get a jump start on next week. Mister B. always appreciates that!"

"I'm sure he does, Betty," said Brogan. "You're in contact with Mister . . . ah . . . Carbariano now?"

"Oh . . . pshaw, no . . . He's probably out whooping up the nightlife. Mister B. . . . . He goes for all kinds of extracurricular activities that just make a girl from Queens *blush*."

"Ah. So you're only in contact with the computers."

"Yeah! Which is why I'm *real* surprised I wasn't aware of you guys coming in, being as I'm plugged into the computers and all—" She made a casual dismissive wave, and a flowery perfume wafted into Brogan's face. "Ah. Doesn't make any difference, really. You guys being cops and all, ain't likely that you're here to steal anything, is it?"

Castle raised her eyebrows in a disbelieving fashion. "Ah—well, actually, that's true. There were a few matters that I had questions about—"

"Yes," said Brogan. "Apparently, there's a whole level of computers that, for some reason, our program wasn't aware of."

"My fault *entirely*," said Castle.

"Be that as it may, we had to come back. We like to be thorough, you know."

"Oh! You must mean the Sideshow Nexus!" said Betty. "You didn't get the Sideshow, huh? Well . . . isn't that just *so* naughty of Mister B.!"

"You know, maybe he forgot," suggested Haldane.

"Could be! Could very well be . . . He forgets to put his guns away all the time! You should see his office! Uzis here, Berettas there. I gotta pick up after him *all* the time."

"Sounds like quite the difficult job you have, Betty," said Castle consolingly.

"Naw . . . It's easy. It's fun . . . I get my kicks where I can, know what I mean, Brogan?" she said, winking broadly at Brogan, sidling up to him, and nudging him with her hip.

"Betty's a receptionologist," said Brogan.

"Yes. I might have guessed," said Castle sardonically.

The irony was lost on the curvy blond android. "Yeah! That's right. They'd be lost without me here. But Brogan, you came to see the Sideshow Nexus, right? Lotsa folks go down there. I don't see why you shouldn't."

"Thanks, Betty."

"Walk this way!" she said gaily, spinning on one of her high heels and launching her formidable prow toward her destination.

"If I walked that way," said Jane, "I'd throw my whole midsection out of joint."

"Yeah," said Haldane. "They sure don't make swivel chassis like those these days."

"So do we follow?" said Castle.

"She's an android hooked up with the system. She's clearly been affected by your program. That's why she's so friendly," said Brogan.

"Goodness," said Castle. "And I thought it was Haldane's winning smile. Let's move it, then. Sounds like a good bet to me, and it may even get us down there free and clear."

They followed the flouncy female android down a hall and then to a stairwell, even as Betty January delivered a nonstop monologue, discussing the dilemmas a young working girl had to deal with in Demeter City.

The stairwell led down into darkness of a strange, pretech dankness. It was as though the foundation of this building had been built many centuries ago. And not here, but on Earth, in the Victorian era, when brick and mortar were the building materials.

Brogan felt as though he was descending into that earlier era now, down into some strange dungeon in the cellar of a castle, not a modern factory on Demeter City.

"Temperature's going down a bit here, don't you think?" said Haldane, unable to contain a shiver.

"A good twenty degrees. Some strains of computers need cooler temperatures to operate."

"I need my long johns I think. These null-suits aren't remotely thermal," said Haldane.

Brogan felt a chill, and not just on his skin. There was something on his spine as well . . . a rime of ice. Their footsteps echoed grimly. It was as though there was some kind of fear generator in place down here.

Whatever it was, it gave Brogan the creeps. He could see that it affected the others as well, in a way they could not quite completely express.

"Cripes, don't you need a flickering torch to guide us down, Betty?" said Haldane.

"Didn't do much ta spruce this part of the joint, up, did they? Ah, don't worry . . . It's pretty nice down where we're going."

"We'll take your word for it," said Brogan.

"That's good. You trust me! You're such a sweetheart! Mister Brogan, I gotta tell you—a girl could get attached to somebody as sweet as you!"

"Well, just trying to be polite, Betty."

"And you *are* . . . and so much more! Here we go. This is a door . . . and oh dear, it's a *good* thing I'm here, because this really isn't accessible to anybody who hasn't got the proper authority."

"Oh . . . goodness . . ." said Jane Castle. "I in particular appreciate that!"

"Oh good! Well then, here we go!" The blond android had at this point attained the entranceway: a huge vaultlike door that would have looked at home in the cellar of some mammoth Fort Knoxish bank.

She focused on the door. There was a click, a whir, and it slowly opened. With her little pinkie, she drew it all the way open, like a game show hostess addressing Door Number Three.

A soft luminescence spilled out, far more enticing than the environs.

"Follow me, then!" she said gaily, and entered spiritedly.

"Well, in for a penny, in for a pound," said Castle. And she strode ahead. Brogan nodded at Haldane and together they strode through the doorway.

More machines.

That was Brogan's immediate impression.

"Come on! This is really the fun part over here!" said Betty, beckoning gaily.

Brogan nodded to the others, and they warily followed the android.

And when they turned the corner, past the metallic, blinking monoliths, Brogan saw exactly what the android receptionologist meant.

CHAPTER

When he was a young man, before he met and fell in love with a Long Island girl named Sally Horton, from time to time Patrick Hogan would take a zip-shuttle down to Atlantic City.

With a date, without a date. With friends, without friends. It made no difference. The experience itself was the charge. Cruising on down to the land with no day, yet eternally lit: the casinos. Here, among the games, he would inevitably ignore the slots, the cards, the rolling roulette wheels, the keno, the other stupidities, including the hot VirtReal gambling that was fleecing the innocent splendorously, and head straight for the craps game.

Ah yes!

Craps!

Ancient, yet contemporary. Dice. Simple as you please, complex as you could want. Come or don't come. Roll the dice. Play the field . . . Boxcars . . . Easy eight.

Seven!

He'd play the game for hours and often win. Not much—it was the play that was the thing, the excitement. The waitress coming up and asking you if you wanted a free drink. The anticipation of the roll. The calculation of probability of the result of spotted cubes of ivory tumbling on green felt. The bark of the stickman, the crazy antics of the bettors as they tried complex and arcane methodologies to win against house rules stacked just enough against them that the casino would always come out ahead. You'd go down to Atlantic City (or Vegas or Reno) and you'd see the holo-displays and the sweeping architecture and the cheesy but expensive shows and it would just tell you who was winning at the metagame. . . . But you'd play anyway, if you had a favorite game, and you didn't lose your shirt.

He hadn't been in a casino for fun for a long, long time. It wasn't a habit you cultivated when you had a wife and a family and a salary you couldn't fool around with much. No big sacrifice, really—he just played on his computer and the occasional VirtReal sim.

Now, though, as Patrick Brogan stepped into the subbasement annex of Mrax Computers, it was as though he were stepping into a memory.

The place looked like a casino.

You had your lights, you had your tables and your red carpeting and special lighting and gambling-inducing smells. You had your slot machines and your keno boards and your vid-poker games, and your penny holo-joys for quick amusement.

What you didn't have now, though, was action.

This particular casino was of the ghost variety.

Empty and still.

"And me without any money!" said Haldane.

"Oooh. You want to play?" said Betty January excitedly. "The house will give you credit, you being a trustworthy member of our friends in blue and all!"

"I'm sure they will, but that's not quite what I meant," said Haldane. He gave Castle and Brogan the eye and Brogan knew what he meant, but was too wise to voice in front of the android. This place wasn't exactly a *legal* gambling den. This place was cause enough for a police raid, cause enough to shut the whole operation down. Gambling wasn't the game that they were after, though. There were deeper things here. Things that they'd have to dig for.

"Ooh . . . Well . . . We've got free drinks, if you like!" said Betty January. "What can I get you?"

"Nothing right now. However, I think Jane might have a question for you."

"Yes . . ." said Jane, quickly and brightly. "Actually, this is all very interesting, Betty, but as I mentioned before we were looking for that auxiliary computer hookup."

"Oh, yeah. . . . That's right. You know what . . ."

David Bischoff

She giggled. "It's right over here, near the Whoopee Room."

"Whoopee Room?"

"You know . . . like naughty holo-sim stuff. . . . The Creons and the Tarns just love the Velcro upside-down party spankings and the squiggle oodles!"

"Squiggle oodles!" said Haldane.

"Sounds right up your alley, Haldane," said Castle. "Actually, Jane, we're not really interested in the Whoopee Room, though we're sure it's quite . . . ahmm . . . first-rate. The computer access, however, *would* be of interest."

"Oh, all right. I'm sure that's no problem to anyone. People here use it all the time."

She led them over to a panel. She hit a button and a full complement of state-of-the-art galactic computer arrays was presented, in a particularly garish neon-light presentation. Indeed, it looked more like a game show than a dead-serious computer. However, Castle seemed to know what to make of it and she stepped forward, rummaged in her little bag of tricks. She halted for a moment, looking at Brogan thoughtfully.

"You know, Lieutenant, weren't you just saying before we got here that you were feeling a little bit thirsty? And aren't you personally interested in alien drink dispensary technology?"

She gave a little arch waggle of her eyebrow.

"Oh, yes . . . Yes, of course," said Brogan. The message was clear enough. Even though she seemed to be totally innocent of this police invasion of Mob property, Castle felt uncomfortable with

Betty's presence while she diddled. Maybe she was going to have to bring out that drill or something. "Betty, I'd love a drink, I think, and if you could show me what kind of bar you have here, that would really please me."

The notion of pleasing Brogan seemed to tickle Betty enormously. "Oh, suuuuuuuuure!" she said, milking the vowel for all it was worth. "Come on! We'll have some fun, Lieutenant Brogan." She beckoned teasingly.

"Just don't have too much fun," said Haldane. "Or I'm going to be jealous."

"Please do remember, however, Betty January," said Castle, "you've got a married man here."

"You think I don't see the ring?" said Betty. "A girl has values . . . Oh, don't worry. I'll take good care of him. Besides, I'm an android! A machine! Right, Lieutenant?"

"Uhm . . . There are times when that can just slip right out of my mind."

"Oh, you're just *so* sweet!" Giggle. "So let's go get that little drinkie-poo!"

"You two call immediately if you need me!" said Brogan.

"Oh, and ditto for you." Castle winked, gave the A-OK sign, and then went back to work, Haldane standing attentively by her side, ready for any heavy stuff—and also acting as lookout.

Brogan brought his attention back to his environs and his guide. Betty led him past a bank of one-armed bandits, jabbering away about some of the parties that she'd been to down here. She seemed totally oblivious to the fact that unregistered gaming like this was illegal. This was her world. Besides, there was also the possibility, as Castle had pointed out, that her program had just blanked the android of that little detail. In any case, it looked as though he was about to get himself a drink, and get an earful of gossip, small talk, and details about some of the throwback operations of this peculiar organization.

When he'd gone to Demeter, Brogan had expected to launch into the future—not take a step back into the past.

They passed a craps table, long and green. A pretty, old fashioned one, quite well maintained. Betty caught him giving it more than a cursory glance.

"You like craps, huh?"

"Oh, I've thrown a few dice, I guess. Not recently, though. No, I'm not a gambler anymore."

"A family man. Oh, isn't that so sweet. You must have a really terrific wife!"

"I'm not about to trade her in if that's what you mean."

"No, I can tell. You're a great guy. You've probably gotta great wife." A little frown. "Me, I ain't had the best of luck. I usually end up with bums."

Brogan didn't particularly feel like going into the nitty-gritty of a female android's personal life, so he quickly changed the subject. He could always talk about the nature of the bums that Betty had bad luck with if they ran out of conversation material.

"That's the bar over there!"

"Oh yeah . . . You are quite the observant one, aren't you? What gave it away? The long serving area? The stools? The racks of bottles and taps?"

"They were all definitely strong clues!"

"You're fun!"

She squeezed his arm playfully, then skipped gaily forward, running around the end of the bar and taking her place in the server's position. "Hello, sir! How may I help you?"

He sat on a comfortable chair. Servomotors delicately engaged, giving him a subtle stim-rub, relaxing him. Well, as long as he was in Rome . . . .

"Just soda and lime, please."

"Nothing stronger?" she said, batting her big lashes with disappointment.

"I am on duty, you know."

"Oh, that's right. Sorry. I don't want to do anything that would get this establishment in trouble, now would I?" She winked and got him his drink. Long tall glass. Ice. A squeeze of lime, dunk of rind. Even as she made it, he could hear the clanking and roaring of Jane Castle's exploratory work. *Bang.* *Screech.* Boy, talk about hacking!

Fortunately, Betty January seemed totally oblivious to anything but him.

"There you go, Lieutenant. A soda and lime, à la Betty." She winked at him. "I'm the sexy babish android with no metallic aftertaste."

Brogan almost sputtered into his drink. "Thanks," he said after a swallow. "Very refreshing."

Betty leaned over toward him in a confidential

manner, exposing an ample amount of her décolletage in the process and filling Brogan's nostrils with her scent. "Your friends don't like me. I can tell."

"I think they like you fine, Betty."

"Pardon me, while I imbibe something a little higher octane." She took one of the bottles, upended it. Amber liquid glugged into a tumbler. She tippled it. "I'm programmed to get sensory input from alcoholic products, in case you wonder," she said. "I don't get drunk. . . . My neural net just jags a bit, making me seem a little tipsy. I'm one complicated unit, Lieutenant."

"I'm sure you are, Betty." Playing along, keeping her talking. He had no idea how long Castle was going to take getting the material she wanted. Better for her to contact him, than to bring Betty back too early.

"People underestimate me, you know, Brogan? Just because I'm a good lookin' dame." The scotch—for that indeed was what Brogan could see that Betty was pouring so liberally—was having a noticeable effect, and quickly.

"Well, you are that—but I dare say you're as well put together on the inside."

"You better believe it, Lieutenant Brogan. They just don't realize how much I do for them at this company. I work just about around the clock. Sure, I have my fun. . . . But sometimes I get the feeling that's my job, too!"

"Having fun?"

"Yeah. I mean, frolicking and partying and

lunching and sitting in people's laps and giggling . . . Well, you know, there's only so much of that kind of stuff that one can do before it becomes work . . ." She hiccuped. "Fortunately, I haven't gotten to that point yet."

"I think it's all right to have fun at work sometimes."

"Do *you*? I mean, have fun at work?" She reached over and played with the zipper device under his chin.

"Certainly."

"I'm glad to hear that, Brogan. All work and no play makes a dull boy. What's your first name . . . no . . . let me see if I can guess . . . Why, Patrick!"

"Yes. How . . ."

"We've got access to public records. Your first name is certainly public record, right?"

Brogan could only nod. He wondered what *else* was public record. What else did this curious person know. The way she was looking at him now, she seemed to be almost fixating on him. She had a dreamy, admiring look on her face . . . almost adoring. It certainly had absolutely nothing machinelike about it, that was for sure. "Uhm . . . right. So I'll know who to call if I want to consult public records."

"Absolutely! So, like I was saying, I get the feeling that although your friends don't like me . . . you do!" She saluted him with her tumbler, drank up some more.

"I can only vouch for that last part, Betty." He raised his glass of soda water and lime.

"I'm glad, Patrick. I really am glad. So tell me something sweet about yourself, something real secret . . . and I'll tell you something about myself."

"Well—my wife and I are very much in love."

"And you've got two adorable kids and all that . . . I know, I know . . . Tell me Patrick Brogan . . . What's your biggest fantasy?"

"A good life for my kids, I guess. Happiness for all races of the Universe? Does that fit your needs?"

"That's *not* the kind of fantasy I'm talking about, guy." She was slurring her words. She stared at her tumbler, clearly confused. "This stuff is *strong*! It certainly doesn't usually affect me like this."

"You can't just alter your programming operations?"

"Normally I can, but something's wrong." She blinked, then walked around the bar, holding on to it for support. "Something's *real* wrong, Patrick."

Was something amiss with Jane Castle's work on the computer system? Had she accidently dropped a spanner into the gizmo?

The blond android woozily staggered toward him. "I'm . . . feeling . . . so . . . weird . . ."

Before Brogan could say or do anything, Betty January fell and he found his arms full of surprisingly accurately formed and feeling female.

"Betty . . . Betty . . . wake up . . . Damn!" Brogan dragged her over to a lounge couch, draping her over the side. This android's programming was amazing! She fainted exactly like a live biological woman would—perhaps, if anything, rather more delicately. She felt warm and soft to the touch—vulnerable.

Her bosom swelled sweetly.

He patted her cheeks. "Betty?"

What would that do? Precious little. She was synthetic, not real, living flesh. He couldn't expect . . .

"Hey dere! Copper!"

The voice brought him up and around. Behind him stood the imposing form of Vinnie Carbariano. He wore a long coat draped over his shoulders. A cigar was clenched in his teeth.

A tommy gun pointed at Brogan.

"Got somethin' for ya here, Brogan!"

The tommy gun spoke.

CHAPTER

Jack Haldane watched
Jane Castle's perfect rear end wriggle at the mouth
of the opening in the computer casing.

Good view.

"Hey there! Need some help?"

"I'm doing fine here. I'm . . . oh!"

"You okay?"

"Damn. I can't quite reach that coupling.
Haldane, you don't suppose you could grab hold of
me and make sure I don't go teacup over saucer
here while I reach?"

If there had been a camera around, Jack
Haldane would have grinned at the audience.

He stepped forward, carefully took both hands,
and placed one on each side of Castle's posterior.

Ah! How he'd *dreamed* about this!

"Gotcha! Make your move!"

He positioned himself behind her, holding on to give her the balance to move forward. The feel of his hands upon her haunches was not an unpleasant sensation.

Jack Haldane had come to an unpleasant realization once he'd arrived at the Demeter Precinct space station. Quite simply, there weren't as many young women here as back home. He was in a position to break free of the shackles of Earth, since he'd just broken up with a longtime girlfriend, Julia, who worked on Wall Street. However, at the time, he was simply tired of women. The attention of females was something that Jack had never had to worry too much about, because of his sharp, clean-cut looks, his strong athletic frame, and his way around a smile. So when the opportunity came of taking his show not merely upon the road, but into outer space, he snapped at it. If some antediluvian section of his R-complex had asked—"Hey—what about babes!" his ego must have swiftly answered, "Ah . . . I'm going to have my pick of any women there!"

Unfortunately, he hadn't realized A) There would be precious few single women who wanted to check out the galaxy. True, the situation was getting slightly better, but even so the ladies weren't exactly beating down his door. B) He would get a crush on the one truly beautiful woman he'd ever met, and she had about as much interest in him as she might have in a gnat.

Well, that wasn't *quite* true. Jane Castle at times seemed fond of him—but a fondness that seemed more like that for an imbecilic brother than for a hot, sharp stud like Jack Haldane.

Good thing he had a sense of humor, or he'd be seriously despondent. Now, though, with his hands on her he was touching previously forbidden territory, and that was a new sensation for Jack Haldane, and he rather reveled in the thrill.

"Damn. Can't quite reach it. You want to lower me a bit, Haldane?"

Haldane grabbed her thighs, scissored her legs, and gently but firmly lowered her.

"That's good. Yes. Perfect. Got it. Hey, you're pretty good at this."

Haldane looked down at this interesting perspective, his torso between her spread legs, hands clamped down over her strong thighs.

"Practice," he said.

"Enjoy it while you can," she said, and he almost dropped her. He felt a ripple in her as she yanked and fidgeted. "There. Now, I'll have to rely on your manly might. Haul me out."

The light from her illuminator streamed and bounced as he brought her back out of the computer maw.

"Was I gentle enough?" said Haldane.

"Oh, you're everything a girl could want in a man," said Castle, mockingly. "If she wants to do a CPU dive, that is. Thanks." With no further ado, she attacked the peculiarly ergonomic keyboards. Bits and pieces of this and that, color and monochrome, flew across the screen, reassembling into something that Haldane could make neither hide nor hair of, but seemed to be of great interest and satisfaction to Jane Castle.

"My goodness," she said. "I've never seen anything like this before . . ." she whispered. "It's *huge*. And it's just amazingly intricate."

"What . . . the computer system . . . ?"

"Yes, and there's something more going on here. There are programs here for things I've never seen before."

"Alien programs?"

"No. All the languages are quite conventional. Advanced, and state-of-the-art, but conventional. No, it's what they're for I'm not entirely sure of."

"You're recording here?"

"Oh, absolutely. I'm getting this all charged onto my cube. We're going to have plenty of evidence here. I mean, as though this casino isn't enough, this material is going to open this place up wide for a legitimate police clampdown. Mrax Computers is going to look like a cop convention next week!"

"Say. Easy stuff. Lots easier than we thought it would be, Jane. I figured an all-nighter, easy. Hey—what about a drink at my place afterward. I've got just the greatest set of the new regressive cocktail rock shipped in. We could catch some tunes before anyone else in this system."

"Thanks, Haldane. I'd truly enjoy maintaining this intimate connection we've established . . ." She winked him. "I've got a standing date with my pillow, though. We've very close. Besides, I'm not a regressive kind of girl."

"Say, we should get together for dinner though sometime, and I'll turn you on to some really interesting stuff. *My* tastes are entirely catholic—food and music both, and I'm sure we can find *something* that you like."

"Oh, you know I like a lot—but somehow I don't think I'd like them entirely with that Haldane spin."

"Hey—you like the precinct house with the Haldane spin. In fact, it's positively centrifugal."

"Yes, but I'd just prefer not gravitating your way, Jack." She beckoned him to help her put the casing of the console back into place.

Haldane did so happily. Yes, she could protest all she wanted, but deep down in her female whatever, he could feel something wet and warm. . . . Anyway, whatever happened now, absolutely nothing could take away this delectable hands-on experience he'd just had. She wouldn't admit it in a million years, but she probably had enjoyed it as well. Perhaps she'd even invite him to go Dumpster-diving with her sometime, heh heh.

With her special device, she resealed the thing, then checked the results on the monitor. "Yes. That should be enough." She popped the cube, put it into her sack. "We've got enough to incriminate a small army here, and we can get the rest later. Now we've got to get Brogan. Glad he took Miss Boobuary off for that drink, but where the hell did she take *him*?"

"The bar, I'd venture to say."

"Brilliant guess. We'd best go and collect him.

I'll follow you, Haldane. My guess is that you've more of a nose for bars than I do."

"Not real hard finding a bar in a casino. Usually it's in the center of the whole thing."

"Let's go find it, shall we?"

They were about to step along in that direction when a voice interrupted them in their progress.

"Say, youse two."

Haldane turned, gun out and ready.

Something whacked his weapon out of his hand. When Castle tried to draw her weapon, the same thing happened.

The monitor erupted into the face of a man in a black hat, slouched down over beady eyes.

The computer console had grown elongated hands, with which it had batted away their guns, and which now looped around their midsections like the tentacles of some angry octopus.

"Welcome to the Linguini Zone. No guns allowed. Look—dere's a signpost straight up ahead. It says 'Your Ass is Grass.' Pucker up, lovebirds. Be seeing ya."

The arms hurled Haldane into Castle, hard enough to knock them both out.

The close proximity was not the pleasurable experience that Jack Haldane had hoped it would be.

The tommy gun spoke.

"Welcome to the Linguini Zone," it said. "Be seeing ya."

An energy burst connected gun nozzle to Patrick Brogan's head.

For the moment, the Universe seemed to freeze . . . And then it slowly faded to a black tarry substance that smelled a very great deal like unconsciousness.

The morning came in like treacle—oozy and far too light.

Patrick Brogan was first aware of this light, and that he viewed it from his head, which was plunked down on a blotter atop a desk. In front of his nose was a shot glass, half-full, with his hand wrapped around it. In his other hand was a fifth of Jack Daniel's—

From the headache and the grime on his tongue and the churning in his stomach, Brogan could only assume that he'd drunk the other four-fifths the night before.

"Uhh," said Brogan.

Pushing himself up off the desk was like one of the labors of a pregnant Hercules. He eased himself up and peered around blearily.

He was in a spartan office, and it was all Greek to him.

There was a couch, a coffee table, some magazines, a hat and coat rack, wood floors, a cracked mirror, another desk with an ancient rotary phone atop it. A door with frosted glass and backwards letters.

Brogan struggled to make the letters out.

PATRICK BROGAN, they said. PRIVATE INVESTIGATIONS.

What the hell—

The door opened, and Betty January came in carrying a brown paper bag.

"Good morning, Mister Brogan," she said in a piping, singsong good morning voice that was like teacher's chalk upon Brogan's slate-heavy brain. "Big day today. How are you?"

"Not so good—" he said, leaning into his hands. "I don't understand a damn thing that's going on."

That wasn't quite true, but it was close enough. His memories were like the sludge at the bottom of the Hudson River—murky and muddy. Something about being a New York cop on an alien planet (what a bizarre concept!). Nothing much about being a detective, that was for sure.

Betty January tsk-tsked. "Oh dear, you've been drinking again, Mister Brogan. And it's that awful war wound."

"War wound?"

"That's right. WWII. That's what gave you the plate in your skull, right?"

"Plate in the skull?"

"Well, I've got something to fix you up just fine. In this brown bag here I've got a great big cup of java with milk, just how you like it. And one nice Danish from Heinman's Delicatessen down the road. Strawberry!"

Brogan managed to hoist himself up and drag himself over to the cracked mirror he'd noticed before. He peered into it, almost afraid of what he'd find.

What he saw was a face. His face, most assuredly, but with an addition. Horn-rimmed glasses. On either side of the glasses, soft red lights blipped sequentially, like landing lights on an air car. He tried to take the glasses off, but he couldn't. They were stuck. There were wires that connected the stems of the glasses to hearing aid–like devices in his earlobes. Plus wires that seemed directly connected to brainlobes via holes.

No wonder he had a headache!

Brogan felt a rush of anger and indignation. What had they done to him? (What had *who* done to him?)

"Mister Brogan. Here. Have some coffee. It'll clear your head up! You'll feel much better."

Brogan was immediately aware of a large paper cup of coffee getting thrust under his nose. The aromatic smell of fresh coffee was familiar and homey, and the headache seemed to lessen. He took it and sipped. The warmth suffused his face and his body, and the taste was like ground heaven. The caffeine immediately jolted him into another dimension of consciousness.

"Mrax Computers," he said. He looked at the woman who'd given him the coffee. Betty January, in more of a business suit now: the efficient Earth secretary, circa 1940s. "And Betty—you're an android."

"Oh sure, in real life . . . but right now, I'm your faithful assistant. And you're Patrick Brogan, P.I. And we've got a mystery to solve today . . . I guess. Let me consult my appointment pad." She handed

Brogan the bag holding the strawberry Danish and hurried over to the small desk in the corner, where she whipped open a neat little book and drew her finger down a page.

"The Maltese Falcon," she pronounced carefully. "No . . . That bird flew last week. The Hound of the Baskervilles. Nope, that's in the kennel . . . and wasn't that a bitch of a case! The Lady in the Lake . . . She was all wet if you ask me . . . Ah! Here we go. Ten A.M. Mysterious Woman in Black . . . Gangland Scandal . . . Mafia Showdown . . . Gee, Mister Brogan, you've got yourself *one* busy day!"

He bolted some more coffee, took a bite of the Danish. He stumbled to the desk, opened a drawer to put the whiskey away . . .

And that was when he saw the gun.

It was a .44 Magnum . . . black and deadly . . . He touched the cool grim metal. Images flashed through his hand, straight to his visual cortex with photoelectronic urgency:

A woman, curly-haired, loving . . . Sally.

. . . a gun . . .

. . . a face . . .

. . . a warehouse . . .

. . . a blast of fire . . .

. . . a fallen body . . .

. . . carried out by cohorts . . .

More: Podly's big, mug—bizarrely and uncharacteristically grinning.

Two children—playing . . . his children, he knew by some parental sixth sense . . .

Liz and Matt. The names floated into his awareness, and he felt paternal love and protectiveness toward them.

Other images erupted . . . forcing out the initial visions.

He saw skewed streets, stark and sepia. Old cars with internal combustion engines wheezing out plumes of exhaust. He heard the rat-a-tat of machine guns, and the hubbub of a different era. He was washed with images of hitting the beaches at Normandy, of a war in France against Nazis—

Of a different life than his, tacked onto a P.I. license and a gun, that was overlaid on his like a patchwork suit.

"I'm Patrick Brogan, Private Investigator," he said, as though getting the feel of the concept.

"Well of course you are, silly!" said Betty January. "The best private dick in New York City. And we're not just talking dick and jane here!" She tittered at her feeble joke.

His mind rebelled. "Wait a minute! I'm not a private investigator. I'm a cop." He went to the window and peered out. He saw a New York street filled with Model A Fords and Plymouths and other twentieth-century cars. He also saw skyscrapers, the Empire State Building prominent among them. But this was nothing like anything he'd ever seen in the movies. The buildings looked tilted, out of kilter and sketched—as though they were the work of matte artists who majored in Warner Brothers cartoons. These buildings looked as though they were tempted to come alive and start singing "On With the Show—This is It!"

"Don't be silly, Mister Brogan. Now just settle down and eat your Danish and drink your coffee. You'll feel much better. Don't forget. Mystery woman at 10:00 A.M. You gotta excuse me, I gotta powder my nose in the little girls' room." Betty January giggled, wiggled her fingers in a toodle-oo kind of way, and sashayed out of the office, closing the door behind her.

His headache was clearing, but it wasn't making life much easier. Confused patterns of thought ran through the field of his mind like football players with dirty cleats.

He went to the couch, sat down, feeling dazed.

On the coffee table was a copy of the *New York Daily News*. A picture on its front showed a pair of bodies lying on a sidewalk outside a Little Italy cafe.

BULLETS FOR BAD GUYS, said the headline.

He lay down and closed his eyes, cutting out all the sensory array around him, focusing on the image and notion of himself as Patrick Brogan, cop, not Patrick Brogan, P.I. Somehow these glasses were creating some kind of different reality . . . But how? And why? And how did this different reality seem so absolutely *real?*

His musings were interrupted as the door opened. He heard footsteps click across the wood floor. He opened his eyes in time to see the back of a woman in a sleek black suit and silk stockings sway enticingly toward his desk, trailing the floral scent of expensive perfume.

Around her shoulders was a mink wrap and in her sleek gloved hand was a cigarette in an ivory cigarette holder. She wore a black hat with a mesh net veiling her eyes. She had long, perfectly combed brunette hair.

The Mystery Woman in Black.

She inspected the desk and looked as though she wanted to go through the drawers.

"If you're looking for Patrick Brogan, he's sitting on the couch," he found himself saying.

She swung around and smiled at him alluringly. "Hello, there. I've come with a message from a certain somebody." Her voice was cultured and cool, a sexy contralto.

Brogan blinked, stunned.

It was Betty January.

"Betty!" he said. "What are you doing in that wig and that outfit?"

"Betty? I don't know what you're talking about. My name is Alicia. Alicia van Dorn."

"You just walked out of here. You must have changed!"

"Mister Brogan, I don't know what you're talking about . . . now, may we please get on with the script!"

He was tempted to go over yank off this new wig of hers, but he wanted to know what she had to say.

"You have a message for me."

"Yes. And it involves all the people you really care about! And a person from the past." She stalked over and sat by him, placing her cigarette in the ashtray. The next thing he knew, she was in his arms, kissing him.

The sensation was not unpleasant, but a tongue in your mouth when it isn't yours is a startling sensation indeed. He pushed her away, but she clung like sandwich wrap. She had all the bits and pieces that made being close to a woman so terrific, and the fact that she smelled so good and looked so good and was the best thing to happen to Brogan this whole (possible) dream segment. Nothing hurt anymore. In fact, everything felt pretty damned good.

Unfortunately, there was one little detail that he had to remember here.

"Uhm . . . I'm married."

"Not in this reality, you aren't. You want to show me a ring?" Her glove smoothed down his face—silky sensation. Her other glove ran down his back and spine with perfect pressure. She squooched against him provocatively, and senses Brogan didn't even realize he had went off. "I can't help it! I find you *sooo* attractive."

This woman knew a guy's nerve endings!

He was finding it hard to speak, let alone do anything else, but somehow he managed to disentangle himself and gently push her away.

"I'm sorry. You said you had some important information."

"God, you don't *act* like a stereotypical private eye!" She rearranged herself. "Oh well. No sense in getting involved with a dead man."

"Oh? I haven't read my newspaper obituary yet."

She got up, gave him a cool gaze. She unbuttoned the top of her business suit, reached in past some frilly underthings. He was about to protest, when she drew out an envelope and shoved it at him. "Here. Take it. Read it. I was sent to give this to you."

Without further ado, she stormed out of the office, rebuttoning her blouse as she hurried.

He took the envelope, opened it.

Inside, a card read:

THE PLEASURE OF YOUR COMPANY IS
REQUESTED FOR LUNCH AT NOON.
RIGOLETTO'S—MOTT STREET

Sincerely,
Dominick Monteleone.

CHAPTER

Normally, Jack
Haldane was never particularly crazy about waking up. Especially when his head felt like it had been used for a clapper inside a cathedral bell.

However, as consciousness dripped back through him like a rainy dawn, and he opened his eyes, he found himself lying on a bed of soft grass, arms wrapped around a beautiful woman, his mouth touching her lips.

He could not help himself: instinct took over.

He kissed her.

She was wearing some kind of black horn-rimmed glasses, but there could be no doubt who she was. Jane Castle.

She moaned, moved against him, responding to the kiss.

Her eyes fluttered open, then fastened upon him

with growing intellectual comprehension and horror. She been kissing Jack Haldane and she had *liked* it. Her body had been close to his and had betrayed her: it had responded to him!

"Blecch!" she said, and pushed away from him.

"Sorry," he said. "I just couldn't stop myself."

She was trying to move away from him, get as much distance as possible, and Haldane was so confused he didn't do anything to prevent her. However, immediately his right arm was pulled up and dragged after her. It wrenched to a halt, and so did Jane Castle. Metal bit into Jack Haldane's wrist.

There were connected by a set of handcuffs.

Jane's hair was disheveled. She looked at the handcuffs with disbelief. "What the bloody hell are these . . . ?" She whipped her head around. "What are we doing here? Last I remember we were in a casino!"

Haldane's memory was close to blank on that one as well. He remembered the casino all right, and he remembered his partner, Patrick Brogan. Something about something . . .

He shook his head. "Well, looks to me like whatever's going on, we're in Central Park."

"Or a strange version of Central Park, anyway," said Jane. "What are these?" She reached up and tried to take her horn-rimmed glasses off, without success. "Damn. They're wired in. We've had some kind of bizarre operation here."

With his free hand, Haldane felt the arrangement of his own glasses. "Drilled right into the skull, feels like."

"Some kind of Virtual Reality modulators?" she wondered.

"Well, if they are, they're astoundingly accurate. I mean, I've never felt anything as real as these handcuffs. And I gotta tell you, Castle, if that kiss was Virtual Reality, I'm getting married to a Virtual Girl!"

Castle blushed a bit. Haldane did not mention her reaction, merely cherished it. Looked like she felt that kiss was pretty damned authentic as well.

"Central Park. Some kind of combination of Virtual Reality and true reality. But why?"

"You know, whenever I think, a New York cop on an alien planet, I ask myself that very same question."

"Let's not get into depth psychology, here, Haldane. We're in, as you New Yorkers like to say, a pickle!" She rattled her handcuff. "And a Hitchcockian pickle as well!"

"I thought it was a kinky pickle."

She shot him a nasty look. *The 39 Steps*—Robert Donat and Madeleine Carroll . . . they were handcuffed together. Film from the late 1930s."

"Man. Mondo bondage!"

"Haldane, your education leaves something to be desired."

"Educate me! Desire me!" He looked up. "Okay, I'm a practical sort. We're in a version of Central Park in a version of New York. . . . We're handcuffed and we're not crazy about that. First thing we do, we gotta get the handcuffs off. As I have no keys, may I suggest that we find a hardware store and get ourselves a hacksaw?"

"Now there's a practical suggestion, Haldane. Seeing as you're a New Yorker, perhaps you have an idea of where the closest hardware store is?"

He looked around and got his bearings. "Okay, we're about level with Eighty-fifth Street. We can go East Side or West Side, but I'm pretty sure the closest is about on Amsterdam on the West Side."

"That's where we're going then." She hopped up and tugged at him. "Up and at 'em, cowboy. This world may not be particularly brave or particularly new—but we have to deal with it, don't we?"

"Yeah. You got that right." He pointed through the field past a bunch of trees. "That should be the road through there that puts us out on the other side of the park."

Even as he was hoisting himself up, he heard a crack. Something hard smacked into a rock near his foot, richocheting away.

A bullet!

Instinctively, he reached for his own gun, wheeling around to determine the direction of his attacker. His gun was gone. Castle crouched as well. He could see no one.

"That way!" he cried, pointing toward the thick copse of trees. Castle did not need to be coaxed. They ran for the woods. More bullets smacked at their heels.

Breaths ratcheting and hot in his throat, Haldane finally pulled them around the thick bole of a sycamore. He peered out carefully. The hail of bullets had stopped.

He could see no sign of any shooters.

"Coast clear," he said.

"Who the devil was shooting at us?"

"Hard to say. Those bullets seemed real enough."

"Indeed. I heard one ring right past my ear!"

"Funny. I had the exact same sensation."

Jane looked about warily, obviously not at all comfortable with walking between trees when they had just been shot it. "Bit of the paranoid scenario, this. Why would they want to kill us?"

"Something's coming back to me. We were tapping a computer. You stuck the crystal cube in your sack. We had information on that cube. You still have it?"

Jane still wore a sack. She reached in. Pulled out the cube. "Yes, as a matter of fact, I do!"

It sparkled in her hand.

"That's what they're after. It must be. We're cops, remember! We broke into Mrax Computers."

Jane put the crystal cube back and rubbed the sides of her gogglelike glasses. "And they broke into us, from the feel of it!"

"Whatever the background situation is, it'll be a lot easier on us if we can get these cuffs off."

She shook her head. "Whoever came up with this scenario has a malicious sense of humor."

"Let's just hope this version of New York has Mack's Hardware like the one I remember. C'mon. We can't just sit here in the park and neck. I've had my way with you anyway."

He started walking, and, with no choice, she followed.

"I hope you enjoyed it, because it won't happen again!" Jane said.

"C'mon, Jane. Let's be real. You enjoyed it as much as I did." Warily, they made their way through an open field, toward a road.

"I did, did I?"

"Hey, I've kissed a few women in my time. I know when they respond and when they don't."

She smiled at him knowledgeably. "Believe me. You'd know it if I *really* responded. Of course, you'll never get a chance to discover that anyway. Besides, Haldane, I don't go for ménage à trois."

"Ménage à trois?"

"Yes. You, me—and your inflated ego."

"Oh, but you'd like the other inflated parts of me!"

"Like your lungs—with hot air!"

They had reached the road. It wasn't a city avenue, but rather a park road that wound from a tunnel on to the tall apartment buildings of the West Side of New York. A slight summer haze hung over them, and a balmy breeze rustled the leaves of nearby trees. The air here smelled of dirt and fresh asphalt.

A noise rumbled from the tunnel.

"Hurry," said Haldane. "Behind that tree."

Castle did not object.

From behind the large bole, they peered out.

Rolling along the road was a Plymouth roadster, complete with running boards and bumpershoots. A man wearing a hat was behind the wheel, wearing a costume that was definitely of period quality.

It rattled along and disappeared among the trees.

Haldane and Castle looked at each other bemusedly.

"Central Park, mid-twentieth century!" said Haldane. "Roaring twenties?"

"Nineteen-forties I'd say."

"Odd. I like those old cars. That one looked like an old combo of twenties and forties."

"Let's go find out, shall we?"

Along the side of the road was a sidewalk. The two of them navigated this for a while in silence, keeping an eye on traffic and pursuers with guns. They had no problem, and they reached Central Park West within minutes.

Passersby walked and women pushed baby carts. Traffic cruised along. All this was of an unusual blend of not only the twenties and forties, but other eras as well—albeit, from what Haldane could see, all from the twentieth century.

"Say, these 'cuffs are going to be kind of conspicuous," said Haldane. "Unless . . ."

He grabbed hold of Jane's hand.

"Well, you *are* getting your jollies today, aren't you?"

"A guy gets them where he can, especially on an alien planet."

"You know, the Tarn women aren't too bad. I've seen a couple looking your way at the office."

"No thanks. Reproductive incompatibilities aside, I wouldn't care for a telekinetic relationship."

"You don't want to float in the air about a girl, Romeo?"

she snapped tartly.

"I've gone down too many times in flames over you."

"Oh, isn't this romantic?"

Haldane wished it was. In fact, it was anything but. However, he was glad that Castle was with him. He had the feeling she was going to be more than just a good companion. Whatever this place was, it wasn't good, even if the park smells and the fumes from auto and the smell of sauerkraut from that hot dog vendor on the corner were familiar.

They found themselves on Eighty-fourth Street, West Side. You could almost see the Hudson River from here. Haldane led her down in the general direction of Broadway. But they didn't have to go that far. They crossed Columbus with the light, then walked the block down to Amsterdam.

Another block south, and Haldane was smiling.

"What do you know! I was right. I thought that Mack's store was old!"

There it was, looking much newer and spiffier under a latticed network of fire escapes.

MACK'S HARDWARE, with freshly washed plate-glass windows and wooden framing, showing off sales displays.

OPEN, declared a friendly sign.

"Come on," said Haldane.

Together they entered the door. A bell jangled as they entered. It was a small store, with narrow aisles. The shelves were jammed with the usual nails and tools and paint cans. It smelled of floor wax.

"Hacksaws," said Haldane. "Over here."

"Do we have money?"

"Hey. We're cops. We get privileges." What he hoped he could do was just to use a hacksaw in the store.

However, even as they were perusing the tool hangers, a voice erupted from behind them.

"Can I help youse two?"

They turned around.

Standing there was Vinnie Carbariano, grinning.

CHAPTER

Patrick Brogan took
a cab down to Little Italy.

He figured the subways wouldn't be bad, but
he'd found plenty of money in a petty cash box in
the desk. Cabs were faster, probably safer.

Yeah, he thought, getting out at a corner by a
fire hydrant. As though "safe" meant anything in
these odd, skewed, anachronistic streets. He'd seen
several decades' worth of styles here on humans—
and aliens. Not just Tarns and Creons either, but
things Brogan had never seen before.

Brogan had left the card he'd received. But he'd
brought the gun. It had comfortable heft and
immediacy in his belt.

Monteleone.

Dominick Monteleone.

Alive? A note from an old foe in the middle of an

old city that had the definite air of nonreality to it did not necessarily constitute the return from the dead of Dominick Monteleone.

However, whoever was in control here, whoever was playing games with him, knew about the past. His past, his city's past, his country's past—

Knew they were putting the past into the future, with a deadly twist, a sarcastic dose of poisonous oregano.

The cab let him off on a curb unusually clean for New York City. He peeled off money from a roll and handed it to the cabbie, a guy with a Brooklyn accent who'd complained about all the different races coming into town. *Just wait around for a while,* thought Brogan. *They'll be driving your cab—and a sight better than you!*

The restaurant was bright and cheerful, with curlicues in the signage. The weather was warm enough for alfresco dining. Couples sat at sidewalk tables, sipping espresso and eating biscotti or pastries. Cigarette smoke dribbled out toward the street, which smelled of fruit and vegetables from a nearby fresh produce stand.

Brogan touched his nose. He could *smell* all this input, yet there wasn't any kind of device inserted in his nostrils. Just how *real* was it?

The rich smells of the restaurant were clear enough as he entered. Meat and cheese and tomato and basil. Waiters in white aprons were bustling about, serving patrons. It looked simultaneously quaint yet profoundly alive, the lines much more organic and traditional than the ones Brogan

SPACE PRECINCT: The Deity-Father

was used to in the twenty-first century. They
harkened back to slower, more ornate times, times
that assumed they would last forever.

A maître d' scurried up to Brogan.

"Patrick Brogan?" he said, peering up above a
curling mustache, below black, slicked-back hair.

"Yeah."

"You are expected in the private dining area in
the rear. Allow me to escort you . . ."

Brogan, eager to keep up the tough guy image,
merely grunted. He held himself tall, tried to affect
the kind of swagger that would be appropriate for
this kind of scene. . . .

Then he told himself, *Hell with it. I am what I
am. I'm a cop, not a private detective.*

In the line of duty he'd been in dangerous situations before so many times he didn't care to count.
If not for his training and his natural instincts, his
number would have been up by now. Whoever was
in charge here, he wasn't going to play by their
rules. The hallway was narrow but pleasantly lit
by electric sconces. The maître d' led him by a
bustling kitchen and a series of oak-paneled doors.
At the very end of the hall, he opened a final door.

"Please. You are expected for luncheon."

The maître d' bowed cordially, gestured.

Brogan entered and the door closed behind him.

He looked around him. He was in a large room,
only dimly lit by candles. In the distance, a
scratchy phonograph was playing Italian opera at
a barely audible level. The room smelled of
antiques, candle wax, and fresh cigarette smoke.

David Bischoff

"Over here, Patrick," said a soft, not unfriendly voice.

By a table covered with a linen tablecloth, a single candle glimmered, cowering before a corner of darkness. The table was elaborately set with the finest of silver, the best of china. A covered basket of bread sticks sat to one side. A salad sat before an empty chair.

Brogan walked over toward the table. As he neared, he saw the candle illuminating only the vaguest of outlines of a figure sitting in the corner, his back against the wall.

Cigarette smoke unwound from a holder, seemingly floating in the near-dark. Twisting through the candlelight, like a languid, lost spirit.

"Bono noche. Sit," said the figure.

Brogan sat.

"Are you hungry?"

"No."

That was the truth. His headache and hangover were gone, too. He remembered much of his past, and he was mentally prepared.

"You should eat. We have an excellent Sicilian meal prepared for you. Some *pesce fresco.* Some nice *calamare. Gnocci.* Perhaps some *finòchio.* You always loved it when I made artichoke and fennel salad for you, *amico.* And then the after-meal drink, *sambucca.* Although I fear you will not get the three coffee beans in your glass this time." Monteleone leaned toward him. "This isn't just a mental exercise, Patrick."

He recognized the voice. A soft baritone with

just the suggestion of a neighborhood accent. Cordial, trained—but wary and cautious. He had not spoken that way when they were students. No, that voice had been higher pitched, more excited, more friendly—awed by the majesty of science and the possibilities of the future.

But then, history and family had interceded.

"This isn't Virtual Reality?"

"No. The chair is real, Patrick. The food is real. Death is real here, Patrick."

"But you. Are you real?"

"I'm not a ghost, if that's what you mean. Oh, I'm real enough, Patrick."

Brogan sat down. Put his hand toward the candle. He could feel the heat against the palm. He kept it there just to the point of burning, then withdrew.

"Yes. Not Virtual Reality. But it's not totally real, is it?"

"Shall we simply call it Real Virtuality? Yes, I think that's a clever term that will do in a pinch."

"So if I pinch myself, that's really fingers manipulating my flesh."

"And pain. That's real. Of course, pain is always real. You know that, don't you, Patrick. You've felt pain before. I certainly have. The whole spectrum. But I digress. Real Virtuality. Yes. We're here. We're having lunch. I'm alive . . . a little more Virtual than Real, alas . . ."

"An overlay of sensory impressions. The whole array."

"Precisely. I have rebuilt my own personal Manhattan, Patrick, in the underground below

Demeter City. Oh, it's not as large as Manhattan—but with the proper mental adjustments the cerebrum implants confer . . . and other modifications which I'll mention later. But yes—my little semimetaphorical fiefdom—my *provincia*."

"So let me get this straight—we're in a room, and there's candles and food on the table. What wouldn't come out in the wash?"

"Hmm? Oh, the music. The candlelight, the oak paneling, the linen, the place settings—and if I turned off your implant, you'd walk through the restaurant and there'd be no one there."

"The mâitre d'?"

"A robot. Under the computer's control."

"Why?"

"The ultimate fantasy is but a gilded reality. That's what we have here, Patrick. But oh . . . there's so much more I need to tell you."

"Don Monteleone . . . Or should I say, 'Virtual' Don?"

"*Bono.* I am to be your Deity Father, my galactic son. And perhaps I shall be the Deity Father to the Universe . . . but most definitely of Demeter City."

"Talk about a crime lord."

A pause. A puff of tobacco that waved out of the darkness like a moiling cloud of gloom. "That's the idea, Patrick. But as I always said, in the latter days . . . crime is a matter of law breaking. And if one has the power to make the law, then the former lawkeepers would perhaps become the criminals."

Brogan picked up a plate. He looked at it. Edged

with gold filigree. He raised it, then smashed it down against the table.

The plate broke as a plate should.

"Are you mimicking Doctor Johnson's refutation of the idea of the insubstantiality of matter, Patrick. Or don't you like the china?"

The figure remained calm, not moving. No hoods came in to rough Brogan up. They hadn't taken his gun. They must feel very much in control here.

"You're dead, Dominick. I killed you."

"So you should apologize, shouldn't you, Patrick?"

"I saw the bullet go into you at that warehouse in the Bronx. I saw you go down. I felt your pulse."

"And you left me, didn't you?"

"I called the coroner's office. I did my job."

"But then the warehouse burned down, and the coroner couldn't get in for my body. It was quite the shoot-out, as I recall. I wasn't the only one who was killed. Couple cops. A few of my men. Ah well. Crime doesn't pay."

"You're not denying you're dead?"

"I'm not denying you killed me, Patrick." The figure leaned forward into the candlelight. He wore an old fashioned tuxedo, rather like Fred Astaire's in *Top Hat*, but he was recognizably Dominick Monteleone. More raffish, perhaps. A debonair touch of gray at the temples. But definitely Nick Monteleone. "However, as Twain said, the reports of my death were greatly exaggerated."

The man was handsome in that unique dark Mediterranean kind of way. Eyes deep as pools of black, a high large forehead, a large, sharp, uncompromising nose. A strong chin below high cheekbones pushing out healthy skin. Dark, strong eyebrows.

Something glimmered now in those pools of dark that were his eyes.

Whatever it was, it wasn't benevolent.

A shiver ran up Brogan's spine.

"What's going on, Nick? It's more than just coming here to be crime lord of Demeter City. More than starting up the Mob again, with you as godfather."

"Is it? Maybe that's exactly what it is, Patrick."

"Something on a larger scale."

"The man nails it! Isn't he smart. But perhaps something else . . . something much pettier . . . but necessary."

Something clicked in Brogan's troubled mind. Connections were made.

"Nanotechnology," he said. "Those little machines . . . Those biotech companies . . . You still own them . . . You're still in control and you've perfected those automated microbes! Wait a minute—back in college . . . You were always touting the theory of the things."

"Very good. This is a test, Patrick. Tell me about myself and nanotechnology . . . You get it right, I'll tell you about the future. Inclusive of *your* future, I might add."

The words tumbled as Brogan put the pieces together. Why hadn't he realized it before? Why hadn't he added the numbers? They'd all been there, fractures of the whole, a jigsaw in disguise. He should have recognized the pieces for what they were, and how they fitted together. He should have recognized them at least by their strange shapes!

"Nanites. I could never comprehend them before, when we roomed at Columbia, Nick. Incomprehensibly small machines. Micromechanics taken beyond the extreme. And these machines, programmed for tasks, could theoretically be implanted in the human body, where they could be controlled for repair work on such small levels that the human body could be healed seemingly miraculously."

"Tsk tsk, Patrick. Not just the human body, of course," said the dark figure, leaning forward, emphasis gleaming in his eyes, the clench of his teeth. "Everything. The very warp and woof of matter, even on a protochemical level. That chair you're sitting in, for instance." Almost casually his fingers stroked the linen of the table. A bubble emerged, flowing from the white to take the form of a miniature control console. Monteleone's delicate fingers danced on the keys.

The armrests of the chair in which Brogan sat flowed up as though they'd become alive. One whipped like a tentacle around Brogan's middle section, securing him fast. Struggle as he liked, he could not move, and his arms were fastened into place. The other whipped up, the end turning into the gleaming steel of a stiletto.

The razor-sharp blade edged across his throat. He could feel its cold, clean, wicked metal.

"I assure you, there is nothing Virtual about the angel of death that hovers near your jugular, Patrick."

"Nanotechnology?"

"Yes. On a scale beyond even my comprehension in my salad days. With the resources and the additional knowledge obtained from contact with extraterrestrial races, the science has grown by leaps and bounds. It is presently merely waiting for the proper usages."

"You wanted me to tell you what happened to you. I can't do that with a knife to my throat, Nick."

"No. Of course not."

A stroke of finger to control. The arms retreated, resuming their previous shape.

The spike of terror that had filled Brogan abated somewhat, but the impression remained. The power inherent in this gesture was amazing. He could not imagine the lengths to which it could be used. But Dominick Monteleone and everything he touched was corrupt and rotten—this kind of knowledge and power would not be used to the benefit of humankind—nor any kind of life at all.

Dominick Monteleone—or whatever Monteleone had become or was going to be—had to be stopped.

"I hadn't realized what you were doing, what you'd done to yourself," continued Brogan. "I knew you still owned companies, but I didn't realize that you'd progressed significantly on your work with nanotechnology."

"All the scientists in my employ didn't clue you in?"

"I wasn't on that level. I was a cop in Manhattan, dealing with street crime. It was your street operations I knew about. The drug dealing, the vice, the whole range of traditional Mafia operations."

"I needed revenue, old friend. You once asked me why I'd done it. . . . Why I'd turned back to my family after all those years of struggling against it. Perhaps I sound like the mad scientist here, but the truth is, the halls of academia and industry in general were turning their backs on me! I was powerless to pursue my dreams. . . . My family came to me and said, 'Dominick. We love you, we believe in what you do. . . . Come with us. We'll give you the money. . . . We'll give you the power to prove out your dreams.'"

"People were in bondage to drugs, to prostitution, to crime and despair . . . People *died* so that your so-called dreams could be realized. Is that worth it, Nick? It wasn't worth it to the Nick Monteleone I roomed with."

"What, back in those misguided, idealistic days when I bought the liberal garbage the intelligentsia dished out while they giggled behind your back? I was a fool then, Patrick. I was only sorry that you went on to become even more of a fool."

"Criminology was always my passion. Keeping the law, enforcing the boundaries that make social life possible."

Monteleone waved his hand in an irritated manner. "Oh, stuff and nonsense. Anyway, you were busy hypothesizing. I'm eager to hear the product of your fertile powers of deduction, Mr. Holmes."

"All that time you were in the crime business, no one noticed the money you channeled into the research side of your organizations. . . . The legitimate companies you owned. . . . And I bet if we called up financial records, we'd discover that each of your companies . . . particularly your biotech and other scientific companies, suffered great losses, because of all the research. They were rather like black holes, weren't they, Nick? Which is why you had to step up the money-making illegitimate side of your operations. The drugs, the extortion, et cetera—to pay for your wild investigations—"

"I had to fund it somehow. . . . You think I enjoyed jumping back into the muck of my ancestors. Do you, Patrick?" The dark eyes glared ferociously. "You despised me for that, didn't you? You despised me after I had so exulted in breaking away from my family, my past—only to slide back. But you see now . . . I had my reasons."

"Yes. And you took your own medicine, didn't you?" Patrick Brogan leaned forward. "You succeeded in your efforts with the nanotechnology—and you injected yourself with your creations. Somehow, they brought you back to life, didn't they—in time to escape from that fire, from the explosion. I remember now. They never found a body. They simply thought you were disassociated atoms, scattered among the debris. But you were alive—in hiding . . . And your companies survived

. . . And when the opportunity arrived to expand to Demeter City . . . you took it. And built. . . . this . . . this crazy existence!"

Monteleone clapped his hands mockingly. "Very close. Very close indeed. Perhaps you should have been a consulting detective, Patrick . . . Not a cop." He leaned forward, scratching his finger thoughtfully against his forehead. "Oh!"

He turned the finger Broganward.

Reached out, pointing.

"But then again . . ."

Brogan could not believe his eyes:

The finger grew out farther and farther from its original state, advancing, its tip finally ending up touching the end of Brogan in a bizarrely admonishing kind of way.

"Perhaps if you were truly a good detective, you would have been able to deduce that much, much earlier in your investigation." He laughed, a faintly manic aspect echoing in the control. "But then, perhaps the whole investigation for this so-called blooming of 'Organized Crime of Mafioso' was in fact a fool's mission. It was so neatly tied up, wasn't it? Perhaps a little too neatly."

"Tell me now, truthfully, ex-friend," said Brogan. "Reality, or Virtuality?"

"Nanotechnology, which falls very solidly into the Reality camp, Patrick."

The finger retracted like an antenna returning to its truncated form.

"Cute trick. Finally popular with the women now, I bet."

Monteleone threw his head back, and laughed. "Oh, I generally have been. Nanotech or not. But we digress." Pause. Close of eyes. As though collecting himself. Brogan noted to himself that Monteleone's little physical trick had taken some physical energy. "We were talking about the great and lauded Organized Crime Crackdown. The End of the Mafia!"

"Clearly we didn't end you. If that's the source of your mirth."

"No! No! Don't you get the joke! Of the all of Mrax Computers! Of *this* for God's sake?"

"Joke? Sorry. I guess I'm just not in a comedic kind of mood."

"Patrick, you sorry old sod. There *was* no Mafia to break down. It was all a sham. Oh sure, we collected enough money to fund my operations. . . . But we had other sources, believe me. The trick was that organized 'crime'—although I truly despise that term—was so legitimate by the time of the so-called 'purge' in which you were involved that there was no way you could truly bring us down . . . it was all a ruse for the other operations of the future . . . a sham. . . .

"It's not about crime, Patrick Brogan. It's about power. Power makes the law, not the lawkeepers."

"The people should make the law, Nick. It should be a consensus."

The dark man shook his head sorrowfully. "I'm not here to debate politics with you, Patrick. And you're not here for any other reason but that I want you here."

"I don't understand, Nick. You *wanted* me to shoot you? You wanted us to think you were dead?"

The man tilted back into the shadows again. His voice deepened with reflection and pain. "No. That was not in the plans. It caused . . . much anguish. Physical and otherwise, Patrick, for reasons you cannot possibly understand."

Brogan let a silence pass, and thought furiously. Even though he had a gun, he felt powerless here. It was not his gun, after all. For all he knew, he could aim it at his tormentor and it would sprout a bouquet of flowers and a little flag that read BANG. This was not a world of his creation. Even though he inhabited it physically, it was not the physicality that he was used to. His only true armament now was his wits . . . and any information he could obtain.

"Why am I here, Nick? Why are you doing this . . . to me."

"Can't you guess?"

"Revenge?"

"I think the proper term for it is *vendetta*, my former friend. My pride, my being calls out for it. But it would give me little pleasure merely to have some henchmen assassinate you. Though that would solve the other problem quickly and efficiently."

"Other problem?"

"The asinine efforts of you and your bumbling rookie partners and that joke of a precinct stand in the way of my plans here on Demeter City. Once you are out of the way, Patrick, I can *buy* your precinct."

"Captain Podly could never be bought."

"Hmm. . . . Pretty much as I thought. Then he'll have to be . . . removed. Replaced with my own Captain." A shadow of a smile. "All this, I know, you would not stand for, Patrick. Which is why I have brought you down here to my little mock-up of twentieth-century New York for the games... but it spans more than this, of course . . . this, my *vendetta*."

"What are you talking about?"

"Just a moment. Show is far better than tell."

He picked up an old-style phone on a phone stand in the shadows. Brogan had not noticed it before, but it was certainly there now. There was the whir of a rotary dialer.

"Yes," said Monteleone. "You can come in now."

Brogan looked around, expecting the arrival of another man in 1940s garb.

Instead, a huge bubble formed in the floor, coalesced into two distinct shapes.

One was that of a kind of alien that Brogan had never seen before. Tentacled. Blobby. Eyestalks waving above a skull and sort of face like seaweed casually touched by an ocean current.

The other was a semiorganic screen on a stand pulsing with subtle lights. It looked more alien than the alien, but the screen itself was a concept with which Brogan was familiar.

The screen showed the inside of his son's bedroom.

Matt was in bed, sleeping, his face softly lit by some unearthly light.

Suddenly, into this view, undulated an arm. A seemingly human arm, attached to a seemingly human hand which held something . . .

A stiletto, like the one with which Brogan had been threatened. And now, like Monteleone's finger, the arm stretched toward Matt's bed. . . .

CHAPTER

Something woke

Matthew Brogan up.

Something scary.

A shiver. The feel of ice inside his soul.

Matt came awake immediately, as though someone had just slapped cold water into his face.

His room was still and quiet, lit only faintly by the glow of his night-light.

The night-light was his principal connection with the earlier realm of his childhood. Matt had always been frightened of the pure dark, of not being able to see even dimly, and his parents always made sure, when he went to bed, that there would be at least one small light illuminating his room.

Now Matt claimed that it was just so he wouldn't trip over any of his odds and ends when he got up to go to the bathroom. His sister Liz could hardly make fun of it: she too had this dread of the dark, and demanded without equivocation an even *larger* night-light than her brother used.

Now, the blocky this-and-that of furniture and books and disk boxes and music stuff and what have you stood like a stolid city of ideas and a testimony to an adolescence-in-progress. The room smelled of the garlic rizzer-chips and grape soda he'd consumed by his computer before he'd gone to bed and of the locker room smell of some old laundry he'd forgotten to give to his mom.

However, even all this familiarity couldn't give him peace.

He felt the presence of *something* else in the room.

He could feel it.

He looked over toward his computer. In the murkiness between him and it there was something different.

As he blinked his eyes into adjustment, he saw that something move. It looked like a very thick rope, the kind of thing that you had to climb in gym class. Only it was stretched out toward him, and at the end of it there was this—

Knife.

As though knowing that he saw it, the knife flicked.

It was a foldout stiletto. It clicked. The blade snapped out, grim and silver, and stood just a few centimeters short of his wide-open eyeball.

"Hello, there, kid. Pleased to meet you," said a somber voice, from the area of his computer. "Let me introduce myself. I'm a man of wealth and fame!"

The computer tittered.

"No!" said Patrick Brogan. "No, don't hurt him. Please!"

A smile twisted on Dominick Monteleone's lips. "That's entirely up to you, of course."

How had this happened?

How had Monteleone gotten control of his son's computer?

The answer came immediately.

Nanites, of course.

A colony of nanites, infesting the material of the computer. But had they been there all this time, waiting for this moment?

No, of course not. They'd just arrived today. . . . In that damned holo-sim he'd let Matt keep.

"Market testing," he spit. "I was such a fool."

"Oh, don't be so hard on yourself. How could you have known?" said Monteleone. "We would have gotten in some other way, Brogan."

Brogan could now see Matt's eyes opening.

Panic filled him as the stiletto opened and threatened.

"Not to worry immediately," said Monteleone. "Actually, I just wanted to get your attention here."

The stiletto blade folded back into its safety position.

The arm withdrew.

The picture faded away into static, but the monitor did not withdraw.

"What are you doing to them . . . ? What's happening there?" demanded Brogan.

"Nothing particularly pleasant," said Monteleone.

"You bastard," spit Brogan. "Your problem is with me, not them. Let my kids be!"

"Oh, not just your kids, Brogan. My vendetta involves your *wife* as well."

He wanted to jump across the table and grip the criminal by the throat, throttle him. However, who knew what defenses there were here. Surely Monteleone would have anticipated such an angry reaction if he showed such a scene to him! Maybe that was what he was milking out of him. Well, he wouldn't have the pleasure!

"Okay. I'm here. I'm listening. What do you want me to do?"

"Play the game, Patrick. Play my little game I've constructed here. It will be *fun*, I assure you. And maybe, just maybe, if you're very amusing and play your role well, your family might survive."

"What about my colleagues!"

"Ah well, we can't have everything, now can we?"

"Where are they?"

"They're in the game, just like you," said Monteleone. "In fact, they're long since out the gate."

"In this bizarre version of New York City."

"Bizarre did you say? Oh, Patrick. I assure you, you haven't seen a fraction of the oddities yet!"

Monteleone laughed.

The screen frizzed back on.

The alien beside it made a sound that could have been a snicker, could have been a death rattle.

On the screen were Jack Haldane and Jane Castle.

In a most compromising situation.

CHAPTER

The blade clicked back.

The elongated arm withdrew, once more becoming part of the base of Matthew Brogan's computer equipment.

However, things did not get better.

"No, Matt," said the computer. "I'm not going to kill you—yet!"

The lights came on.

The computer had somehow changed shape. It now looked like a computer arrangement seen through a fish-eye lens. Squat. Nasty. The CPU suddenly cracked into a mouth, with jagged teeth filed to obscene points. The mouth bent into a leer. A nasty red tongue, dripping saliva, licked the lips.

"Whatcha think about *that*, kid?" said the voice, producing an oleaginous chuckle.

Matt wasn't thinking exactly clearly at this point. He managed to get himself out of bed and, keeping as much distance as possible between himself and his transformed computer, edged toward the door that led to the hall beyond.

He sensed that any moment this computer-thing could pounce. It hunkered and grinned on his desk, like a demon from some mechanized hell.

Suddenly, the monitor came on.

Instead of numbers or letters showing, though, bloodshot eyes glared out.

"I see you, Matt!" said the computer-thing.

Matt shuddered, but kept on walking.

Almost to the door.

The tongue snaked out from the mouth, glided toward him.

Matt smelled a fetid stench as rough pseudoflesh wetly licked the side of his face.

"I *taste* you, Matt!"

Then retreated.

Even as he reached the door, opened it, slammed it behind him, and ran for all he was worth, he could hear the thing chuckling evilly behind him.

If he hadn't been so panicked, he would have pinched himself to make sure this wasn't a nightmare.

He ran down the hall to his parents' room, smacking into the door and hammering away with his fist.

"Mom! Dad! Mom! Dad!"

"Matt?" he heard his mother's voice. "What's wrong?"

That's right. Dad is out on duty tonight! What a night to pick.

"My computer—it's turned into a monster!"

He heard the problem with this statement as soon as it left his mouth. Being an imaginative child, he of course had suffered monsters in the bed, monsters in the closet, monsters in his dinner. Naturally, being an adolescent he'd abandoned that phase. Now, though it was coming back to haunt him:

He was the boy crying wolf!

His mother's voice was sleep-drugged, weary-sounding.

"It's just a dream, Matt. It's probably that sim you got, giving you nightmares. You're a big boy now. Live with it!"

"Mom! It's not! It's *horrible*."

Drat! He should have just said there was a burglar or something. Of course, that was equally unlikely! How could a burglar get aboard a suburban satellite orbiting a planet? And through *these* security measures?

"Of course it is, dear. You want me to go and turn the light on for you? Make you some warm milk?"

Matt heard a *Thump* from his room.

*Thump*Thump.*

"Just *believe*, me, Mom! Maybe it was the sim. But it's really done something to the computer."

There was no time to waste trying to convince her, though.

He had to get some help!

Matt ran toward the nearest comm unit. Stabbed it to life. Unfortunately, nothing happened.

He picked the phone up.

Dead.

The nearest comm unit to this was similarly dead.

Desperate, he ran for the door. The security post was just down the hall. He could summon help there.

He hit the door switch.

Nothing happened.

He tried it again, with absolutely no response.

*Thump*Thump* came the sounds again.

Matt fought down panic. He went to the closet, where the manual override was located. Surely *that* would open the door. He found it, pulled the necessary switch.

Again, nothing.

*Thump * Thump*

THUMP!

"What the heck is going on out there?" he heard his sister's voice demand.

Liz! She was the kind of person who would just fearlessly stalk into his room and demand to know what was going on.

And she'd walk straight into the yawning, teeth-filled maw of the thing.

"Liz. Stay back there. Stay in your room!"

"Hey! What's going on? You can't tell me what to do, Matthew Brogan. I'm my own independent person."

"Yeah, but you can get independently gobbled if you go out into the hall."

"Come on, Matt. You can cut out the nonsense. You're not going to scare me anymore! Not after that little stunt today . . . Not after I humiliated myself—"

She turned the hall switch. Nothing happened—the place was in battery-operated night-light dimness.

"What's going on here, Matt? You know, if you keep on playing these kinds of foolish practical jokes, you're *really* going to get in trouble with Mom—and especially Dad. I know he doesn't believe in kicking kids' butts, but I dare say he'll happily make an exception for you!"

She started walking toward him, wagging her finger demonstratively.

"Liz! No! Don't walk past my door!"

"I can walk where I please, Mister Big Stuff. I truly resent your controlling nature and I'm here to tell you that from this day forward—"

Just as she walked past the door, the door opened.

A green, oozing hulk leaned out, dripping electronic attachments and a lolling, drooling tongue.

"Hiya, cutie? Wanna play a computer game?" it croaked.

"Yiiiiiiiii!" screamed Liz.

She ran down the hall for all she was worth, grabbing and hugging her older brother as though he had abruptly turned into a dashing white knight on a charger.

The creature took a step out into the hall and stood there, wobbling uncertainly, its eyes in the monitor rolling lewdly, its workings squishing obscenely.

"You two!" said Sally, emerging finally from her room, and staring blearily at her troublesome offspring. "You're making enough noise to wake the dead!"

She stood there, arms planted on her hips, looking at them as though she were thinking about having retroactive abortions.

The creature slowly slithered up beside her.

"Mom!" said Matt.

"Behind you, Mom!"

"Oh. Right. You're both in on it, this time, huh? I get it. Dad's out, so you think that this would be an absolutely wonderful opportunity to harrass your exhausted, harried mother. You kids . . . I don't know why we brought you out here. . . . I don't think the Universe is ready for you."

"Mom, the monster . . . it's really there!" said Matt, not knowing any other way of putting it.

"And oh, Mom . . . it's awful!"

"Right. And if I turn around, you're going to just laugh at me and call me gullible. Well, I was born a little bit before you, Matt Brogan. Your sister may be susceptible to your little odd plans, but not me!"

The creature started oozing forward, wiggling and writhing silently.

Matt didn't know what to do.

He sure didn't want to get any closer to the

thing. But then again, this was his mom it was creeping up on.

Who was going to wash his clothes and make dinner for him if she got gobbled?

He ran forward.

"What are you doing, Matthew?"

"Here. Look, Mom." He forcibly turned her around.

The creature that had been his computer was lit from within by an unearthly luminescence. It was translucent, and the dangling bits and pieces that made up its monstrous interior danced in odd syncopation with its gushy guts.

Matt got a whiff of it:

Transistors and computer chips and motherboards risen from the grave.

"Oh," said Sally Brogan. "Very impressive."

"Impressive. Mom! It wants us!"

"Well, of course it wants us. To drag us back to your room and eat our brains, right? I must say, Matthew. That's just about the best hologram I've ever seen."

"Mom! It's not a hologram. I swear. It's real!"

A waggling feeler advanced their way.

"Look, Mom!" cried Liz.

The next thing they knew a goldfish bowl was flying over their heads. It landed square on top of the creature, crashing and letting go its load of water, which splashed down onto the creature.

Exotic fish tumbled. The mouth of the thing opened, the lewd tongue whipped out and lashed two fish simultaneously. Chomped them up noisily.

Belched up the smell of seafood.

"Hi, Mom. Let's party," it said.

Sally Brogan dragged her son away. "Get away from that thing!"

"No kidding!"

They picked up Liz along the way, running out toward the living room.

"Call security!" said Sally.

"Phone's dead."

Sally tried anyway. She threw down the phone with disgust.

They heard the thing slopping along the corridor toward them.

"We've got to get out of here."

"We can't, Mom.

"Of course we can!"

Sally Brogan went through the exact same procedure as her son.

With the same result.

"What's going on? This isn't supposed to happen!"

"I know, Mom, but it has. Dad's got to have something . . . he's always prepared."

"Yeah, like a tank!" said Liz, looking as though she'd like to climb under the rug.

They went back to the living room, and Sally set to work.

"What are you doing, Mom?" asked Matt.

What Sally seemed to be doing was pushing on the couch.

"Help me here," she said.

Matt pushed as well. The couch slid aside.

Below it was a box. His mother banged the box open.

Inside were a number of items. One was a power gun. She pulled this out. Another was an electric flashlight. She pulled this out and turned it on.

The beam of the lamp flicked on just in time for its beam to catch the sight of the creature clumping into the room, vestigial arms outstretched, tongue hanging out lasciviously.

"You know, all I wanted was a safe place for my kids to grow up in," said Sally.

She aimed the gun and fired.

The blast crashed forward and intersected with the creature, dead center. The power of its force blasted the thing back against the wall.

It splattered sparks and less appetizing things. It crashed against the wall, and slipped wetly down into an unspeakable heap of glop and metal and glass.

"Mom! You got it!" cried Liz.

"Good shot, Mom!"

Sally looked at the gun doubtfully. "Whew. Good thing your father told me how to handle one of these things!"

"That wasn't one of Matt's holograms!" said Liz.

"No, I think it can be safe to say that. The question was, what was it? I mean, we've seen some strange things here in this system—but that looked like something out of a nightmare."

"And right in our home. It was from that simulation," said Matt. "It must have gotten inside because of the test marketing sim."

"No wonder it scared the crap out of me! It's still doing it!" said Liz.

"Try the phone, Liz."

Liz went to it, keeping a large distance between herself and the mess that had been the creature. She picked up the phone.

"Matt, try the door again."

Matt went to the door. The electricity was still off, and the emergency opener was on the blink as well.

He reported back.

"Same with the phone," said Liz.

"Well, there's the emergency escape hatch, I suppose."

"Sealed," said a deep, resonant voice.

"What?" said Nancy.

"Who said that?" cried Matt.

"I said that," said the voice.

With a profound sinking feeling in his gut, Matt realized that the voice was coming from the compost heap that had once been the monster that had once been his computer.

The pile stirred.

Rose up like something pushing up out of the grave in an animated movie. . . .

This new formation no longer attempted to resemble Matt's previous computer array, even though chunks of the old CPU stuck out of its lumpish body, and a section of the monitor still formed the head and power cords dangled and lights still twinkled and glimmered within and without. No, now it looked more like a devilish blob of combined protoplasm and pure evil that had swallowed an aquarium and was attempting a sorry imitation of Lon Chaney as the Hunchback of Notre Dame.

Creak. . . .

Splurge. . . .

Squish. . . .

Its voice rose up again, like a loudspeaker slowly bubbling out of a bed of quicksand.

"Don't think you can kill me with a silly gun!" it gurgled with a voice that sounded immensely pleased with itself.

"Well you can bet I'm going to try . . . and damned hard!"

Sally raised the power gun again and squeezed another blast.

This time, though, nothing happened.

"The battery can't be dead," she said.

Matt grabbed it. "Maybe you switched the safety back on, Mom." He held it, checked it. His father had told him about guns, just in case—but he was instructed never to think about even touching one except in case of an emergency. Matt figured this qualified.

However, even as he grabbed the gun and hefted it in his hand, he knew something was wrong.

The power gun was rippling. It felt as if it had come alive, had turned it into a fish just pulled out of a river.

Startled, Matt dropped it onto the floor. Almost instantly, the gun began to change. It quickly mor-phed into a gray puddle—and then the puddle grew pseudopods and wiggled toward the creature. There it was absorbed.

"Ah. A few more quality components to feed me," said the thing. "Thank you!"

"What are you?" demanded Sally.

"Just a moment. Let me get myself a little more presentable."

The thing grew a pair of hyperthyroidic eyes, raggedly rippled with veins. One pupil black, one crimson. Grossly warped fangs sprouted from a knife-tear mouth. Large cancerous warts erupted from its mottled, weirdly translucent skin. Mats of ragged, coarse hair grew in patches. A ratlike tail unwound from its rear. Jagged bat wings erupted from its back, flexed.

Matt caught a whiff of corruption.

"There!" The ragged nose of exposed bone and gristle twitched, testing the air. "Ah. Yes. The sweet warm scent of Earth blood!"

"Get out of my house!" said Sally, defiantly. "You weren't invited. Get out! I warn you. This is a modern domicile. We have all possible security precautions. Sensors have picked up your presence and even now help is on the way."

"Oh no," said the thing. "I don't think so. And by the way, the name is Igor and we're going to have some small amount of time together." It grinned lewdly. "So let me ask you a simple question— What's your favorite movie monster?"

Matt Brogan's blood went cold as the thing gurgled with glee.

CHAPTER

There was a huge
grin on the mobster's face.

Vinnie Carbariano looked totally in his element
now, his duds fairly sparkling with cartoonish
macho.

The handle of the gun in his belt looked
absurdly huge.

"Youse guys having a good time? I see you're
enjoying da kinky addition to your love life!" The
cigar between the man's sneering lips bobbed
obscenely.

"What are you doing with us!" demanded Castle.

"What do you want from us!" Haldane piped up.
He was looking for a stalling measure, buying
time, before the hood could make his move
against them. His eyes cast around for any form
of weapon. They settled on a large stack of paint

cans piled at an aisle's end, the topmost teetering precariously.

"Simple. That little cube ya got. With the computer programs ya leeched out of da mainframe." He winked at Castle. "Oh yeah—and maybe a little fun wit' your heads, too."

"I don't understand," said Jane. "You could have gotten that while we were unconscious."

"Geez—a doll wit' brains!"

"You know, is it hot in here?" said Jane Castle. "Or it me?"

Her jumpsuit had already been unbuttoned to her mid-chest. With her free hand, she unleashed another button, revealing a little more cleavage in the process.

Vinnie Carbariano gawked, his eyes bugging.

Haldane well knew that Jane Castle wasn't the kind of woman to expose an inch of bare skin without very good reason, so he knew the "hot in here" was a cue.

He took the opportunity presented.

Haldane lunged to the right and forward, pushing with all his might at the pile of paint cans. They tumbled eagerly, directly onto Carbariano, knocking him off his feet and almost burying him.

"Hey!" the mobster cried.

"The hacksaw!" cried Haldane.

There was no need. Castle was already reaching for it. She snagged it with her free hand, and they were off, running out of the shop and back onto Amsterdam Avenue.

"Hey! That's shoplifting!" cried a clerk.

"You bums are gonna pay for—" The door slammed on Carbariano's pained yell.

"Where to?" said Castle.

"The park."

"The park? We just came from there."

"The park has bushes and trees. We can hide."

They were already running up Amsterdam. They turned up Eighty-fifth.

"Someone was trying to shoot us in the park."

"And we can get shot just as easily out here. Come on."

Castle made no further complaint. She was too busy puffing along beside him.

At the top of the rise, on Columbus, however, they heard sirens.

"Police! They'll help us," said Castle.

"What? No of course not! This isn't *our* world, Jane!"

"Oh. Yes, I suppose I have entirely unsuitable associations with police here. But it's coming this way, Haldane. Where do we go?"

She was right. Although he couldn't see any car headed their way (and he prayed they couldn't see them either) Haldane could hear that siren get louder. Desperately, he looked around for a place to duck into. No alleys here . . .

However, just a few feet away was a pizza parlor named DINO'S with a large sign in the plate glass window proclaiming OPEN.

"In here!" he cried. He pulled her along after him.

In a matter of moments, they were in the parlor.

Haldane looked around. The place was deserted. No customers, no cooks, no clerks.

However, they were still visible to the outside, and they still had the handcuffs on.

Haldane looked around frantically. There, down that aisle. He pointed. "Come on!"

He nearly dragged her along behind him. "Hey there! Arm out of socket is *not* good."

"Sorry. In here."

He pointed to a door without a handle.

Above it read LADIES.

Castle looked as though she was about to object. A whoop of an old-fashioned siren seemed to change her mind.

"Okay."

They ducked inside.

The door closed behind them.

It was dark. Haldane groped around for the light. He grabbed something a good deal softer.

"I'm afraid that doesn't turn me on either, Haldane," said Castle, sharply.

"Sorry."

He snatched his hand away. He was glad she couldn't see him blush. He groped in a more calculated area by the door. His hand touched the switch. An electric light came on above them.

They were in a small bathroom with a linoleum floor, a sink, a towel dispenser, and a bathroom stall sealed with a coin device. It smelled of disinfectant and hand soap and cheap paper towels.

"You've got the scalpel, Doctor?" said Haldane.

"Yes, but I'm not sure if I should use it on the handcuffs or your neck!" Castle was glaring at him.

"Look. I said I was sorry. Your virtue is safe! I won't tell anyone."

"Just watch where you put your hands next time, huh?"

"Sure. Just give me the saw. We haven't any time to gab here."

She handed him the hacksaw.

Old-fashioned but good enough.

"Okay, now stretch the chain over the sink," he directed her. She obeyed him. He brought the saw up and put the blade to the chain.

Started moving the blade back and forth.

It took a few minutes and strenuous work. Castle bore it like a trouper, even forgetting her quip tendency and encouraging him along in terse but generous praise: "Good. That's it. Excellent job. There you go."

The minutes seemed eternal. Any moment Haldane expected Carbariano, the Keystone Kops, or maybe Margaret Dumont to come crashing through the door.

The link was broken.

They were free.

Haldane put the saw down and rubbed his sore wrist. "Well, we've got some kinky jewelry now, but at least we're free of each other."

"What's that supposed to mean?"

"I mean, now I've got my other hand free."

"So you can grab me again."

"I *said* I was sorry!"

She smiled. "Apology accepted. What next?"

"I wonder if there's another way out of this place."

"Unlikely."

"Back to the front parlor, then." He had a thought. He turned to the cash receptacle for the pay toilet. He kicked it hard. Coins streamed out. "I'm hungry. Let's get a couple of pieces of pizza!"

"So much for law and order!" said Castle.

"Turn me in!"

They went out to the parlor. The smell of cheese and tomato sauce filled the air along with fresh scent of baked crust.

Haldane felt his mouth watering.

There was now, indeed, someone behind the counter.

"Hey dere," said Vinnie Carbariano, grinning above a white apron. "How about some nice-a pizza pie!"

CHAPTER

"Hey dere," said Vinnie
Carbariano on the screen in the Little Italy restaurant in the strange New York City of Dominick
Monteleone. "How about some nice-a pizza pie!"

Patrick Brogan swung around to face his tormentor. "You're toying with them as well," he
snapped.

"But of course," said Monteleone. "I am toying
with you, I am toying with your family—I am toying with your precinct station."

"My precinct station?"

"Licknose? Care to change the channel?"

A tentacle from the hovering alien flicked
around, touched something in the back. A frizz of
static—then a picture slowly filtered into view.

It showed the entirety of the main office of the
precinct station. It was night duty, but there were

still officers there, writing reports or going to the water cooler or doing their other duties.

The view was through a mesh, from the ceiling.

"We haven't taken over there yet . . . but we will. The time will come," said the alien called Licknose.

"How . . . How did you get past security?"

"The dead Creon," replied the alien.

"You don't see yet, do you?" said Monteleone in a condescending way. "No wonder I'm generally several steps ahead of you—with a notable, painful exception."

"Damn! Of course! You injected him with those nanites of yours."

"Very specialized, precinct-storming nanites, I might add," said Monteleone. "Presently building more nanites and ready to take over the station"—he examined his watch—"in about two hours. That will leave Demeter City entirely open to me—and with nanite emplacements already effected it will be just a matter of days before I bring the government to its knees. The spaceport will be mine. . . . With Licknose's help, I have readied shipments of nanites to be spread throughout the known Universe. . . . Soon, perhaps, Brogan, one will be able to get spaghetti with a nice marinara sauce and a bottle of Chianti on Altair 5."

Brogan's mind was threatening to overload. He had to take a step back, relax, calm down. Ask questions.

"Why am I seeing this? If you have such power, why are you playing these games with me? Why not just kill me and get your revenge that way."

Monteleone tapped his fingers on the table. "Oh, I think you already know the answer to that, Patrick. I want you not to only know who your tormentor is . . . I want it to last. . . . But more than that, I want to test you. I want to see what your true mettle is . . . where your loyalties truly are . . . And who knows . . . maybe break you! I could use a person of your caliber. . . . But I get ahead of myself here, Patrick."

"What do you want me to do, Monteleone? What have I got to do to get my family out of your claws?"

"Play a little game of cat and mouse, Patrick. That's all." Monteleone produced a piece of paper, wrote down an address. Passed the paper over to Brogan. "Your friends have an item that we want. A computer crystal of programs, stolen from our computers. They are loose in Manhattan. You must track them down. Kill them. Bring them back. To this address."

"I can't kill them!"

"It's them or your family, Patrick. Your choice."

"But your man—he's got them at that pizza joint. Why not just apprehend them that way?"

"We're leaving that to you, Patrick. You know Manhattan. Enjoy *my* Manhattan. Accomplish your task. Then we shall talk about your family. Understood?"

It was so simple a task.

Yet so complicated.

He got up out of the chair, making no move for his gun.

"I understand. I have no choice. I'll do what you want."

There *was* no choice. He had to humor the madman for at least a while, until something else popped up.

In any event, he needed time to think.

"Good. You've got your gun. I want you to kill those two and bring the computer crystal to this address."

He ripped the page off, threw the paper across to Brogan.

Brogan picked it up.

"This is the Empire State Building!"

"Observation level."

"And who's going to pick up the crystal. King Kong?"

"How *did* you know?"

"I'm going to do all of this with buses or the subway."

"No. I've got a car for you," said Monteleone.

"How thoughtful of you."

"Wait. That's not all! I have a driver as well." He pulled up the ancient phone again. "Okay. You can come in now!"

"I don't suppose it's very easy to appeal to whatever part of you is still sane, Monteleone."

"Sanity is a consensus opinion, Patrick."

"And you're the con with the census here, huh?"

"Quite good. Wordplay is always amusing."

The door opened. There was the click of boots.

"Your driver, Patrick."

Brogan turned around.

Standing behind him was a woman dressed in a black chauffeur's outfit, complete with black hat and black gloves.

A wealth of blond hair emerged from the cap.

"Hi Mister Brogan," said the woman, waving happily, chomping gum.

It was Betty January.

CHAPTER

Matt Haldane, all his
life, had always liked monsters plenty. He had an
extensive collection of crystal movies of all the old
classics. He was a subscriber to lots of monster
magazines and comix, including *Famous Monsters
of Filmland* (edited by the chanelled spirit of
Forrest J. Ackerman).

Matt had monster games, monster vids, monster
books, monster models. He had vampire stuff,
Frankenstein stuff, Blob stuff, and was the number
one fan of the Phantom of the Opera in the
Demeter system.

Now, though, with this . . . this *thing* squatting
lugubriously in the middle of his living room, holding him, his mother, and his sister hostage, Matt's
feelings about monsters were growing rather
ambivalent.

"Who played the Frankenstein monster in the Universal film *Ghost of Frankenstein*, Matt?" asked Igor.

"Bela Lugosi," said Matt, sitting on the couch.

"I thought he played Dracula," said Sally.

"Ah, Mom. Lots of people played Dracula and lots of people played Frankenstein," said Liz.

"Frankenstein's monster."

"And Doctor Frankenstein, too."

"Now, now! Siblings! Behave," said the creature. A bit of glob tumbled from its head, splatting on the floor. Like a globule of mercury, the stuff moiled for a moment. Then it sped back to join the main pile. "You're both right, of course. My favorite Doctor Frankenstein, for instance, was Peter Cushing."

"Mine too," said Matt.

"I'm getting kind of tired of all this," said Liz. "When are you going to let us go?"

The mouth bent into a frown. "But I was having such fun! Oh well, I suppose I can cut your throats now . . ."

Pseudopods grew.

Changed to gleaming cutlasses.

"Ah—no. Maybe that's not the way to go," said Sally, turning a bit green.

"No? Then perhaps—string you up?"

The pseudopods became nooses dangling from tree limbs.

Matt loosened his collar. "Ah—let's play another game, then, if you're bored?"

"Bored? Bored? How can the most interesting life-form in the Universe be bored?" said the creature. "All I have to do is pay attention to myself. Oh yes, I amuse myself vastly!"

"Just what . . . I mean . . . who *are* you, exactly," said Sally, tentatively. "And why are you keeping us here?"

"Me? You want to know about little ol' *me?*" said the creature. The nooses disappeared and the mottled skin of the thing turned a bright chartreuse with pleasure.

"Yes, yes, of course," said Sally. "And what exactly is going on?"

"Me? Just call me Legion," said the thing, "for I contain multitudes.

"Demons?" said Matt.

"Unlikely," said Liz. "This *is* the twenty-first century."

"And what if I were a batch of demons, little girl?" The thing's pseudopods became taloned hands, reaching forward to grasp her. "Come to snatch your soul!"

"Then I guess I'd have to go and get my crucifix and exorcise you!" said Liz defiantly.

"Bah. You're no fun," said the thing. "This biological corporeal form I'm assuming is troubling as well."

"What's your natural form?"

"Hmm? Why, very tiny, minuscule machines, actually."

"I knew it!" said Matt. "Just like the nanites in *The Invasion from Within.*"

"A worthy cinematic effort. But I'm afraid they got the science wrong."

"Nanites?" said Sally.

Liz sighed, clearly frustrated with her non–"with it" mother. "Little itsy-bitsy machines, Mom. The theory is they can go inside you and fix you up. I never heard of them becoming ugly monsters before, though."

"Please!" said the creature. "Beauty is in the eye of the beholder."

"Nanites aren't intelligent though," said Matt.

"What if we're programmed to accumulate and *form* an intelligence?"

"Maybe. But unlikely. Me, I think there's something controlling you."

"Yeah," said Liz, squooching up her face in disgust. "Just like in *The Wizard of Oz*."

"'Pay no attention to that man behind the curtain!'" said Sally, obviously happy to be in the know about something.

The creature purpled. The sides of its face contorted and bulged with exaggerated anger. "You know, I can get very nasty if I want to."

Matt knew it must be true. There was too much personality here to be an instantly fabricated Artificial Intelligence consisting of nanites. Best to keep his mouth shut now, and just watch and see what the thing did.

The funny thing was the security.

Matt knew for sure that this place was *wired*. And the space suburb orbiting the planet had its own security force as well. Matt's dad had made absolutely sure of that, before he'd agreed to come here to live in an environment he knew next to nothing about. Patrick Brogan wasn't paranoid, he was just cautious.

You'd think, with the security in this place, that the guys at the front desk would know *something* was wrong in this particular unit.

On the other hand, maybe they had their own private monster squatting on their blotter, playing Trivial Pursuit with them.

Worse, maybe these nanites were crawling everywhere, transforming this whole suburban vessel into one gigantic space creature, with them inside, Jonahs in jeopardy.

No. Somehow that was a little too large-scale. Whatever was operating that voice, these reactions, it wasn't nanites. Nanites were just machines. Really tiny, dumb machines. Even collectively, they could only operate by programming. There was some central processing unit in this writhing bucket of cartoonish fright that was pulling the strings.

Poke that out, you were in business.

The question was, HOW?

"If you were going to murder us, why haven't you done so yet?" said Matt.

"Matt!" said Mom.

"Oh God, he's going to get us killed for sure!" said Liz.

"I'm perfectly able to paint the walls with your blood! To make sausages with your innards! To hoist your heads on spears! To toss whatever's left into the cold vacuum of space!" said the creature, huffing and puffing.

"Sure you are," said Matt. "But we're not going to do anything that would make you want to or need to. I mean, we're not exactly rebelling are we? We're sitting here trembling and playing the games that you want."

The monster put a pseudopod to its chin thoughtfully. "True. Very, very true."

"So that's what we intend to keep on doing. We're scared out of our minds! We're intimidated and all that stuff. No way are we going to try to escape. Where can we escape to? We're in a space station! Your nanites have got control of everything . . . Haven't they?"

The creature blinked. "Uhm—" Evil, expansive grin. "Why yes . . . Come to think of it they . . . I mean *we* do!"

"So what's the problem! Relax already. You've got us! Give us a little slack, huh? What are we going to do to stop you? You can kill us if you want to, you can play games with us . . . But my guess is that mostly you're just terrorizing us until some sort of decision comes down. And boy, we're really *terrorized,* aren't we?"

He looked over at his mother and sister.

"I, for one, am absolutely terrorized right out of my skull," said his mother.

"Me too! I'm quivering. I'm about to pee myself." Liz started to scream.

"Shhhhhh!" said the monster. "Look, screaming's okay, but only when I want you to scream. You hear?"

"Oh. Okay," said Liz.

The reference to peeing gave Matt an idea.

"Rats. You know, this has all been so traumatic. I need to go to the bathroom, too. I bet you do, too, don't you Mom?"

He nudged her.

"Why . . . yes, of course."

The monster nodded. "So go ahead."

"What—here?" said Matt.

"Sure. Why not!"

"That's disgraceful," said Sally.

"Look, what harm is it if you let us go to the bathroom and do our, uh, duties there. What . . . are we going to climb out the window or something?"

"True. Very true. Very well, little girl. You can go first," said the thing.

"No," said Matt.

"What? I *do* have to go, Matt," said Liz, staring daggers at him.

"No. Don't you remember! We're a family. We do *everything* together." He winked at them.

"Oh. Yes. Right, that's absolutely true," said Sally. "Don't you know that about us humans?"

The creature scratched its head. "I'm afraid my education hasn't been that inclusive."

"Look, there's cheese and lunchmeat in the fridge. And bread and condiments," said Matt. "You go and make yourself a sandwich while we take care of ourselves for a few minutes. Then we'll meet back here and you can continue terrorizing us."

The monster nodded. "Yes. That sounds fine . . . You're quite correct. It's not as though you can escape from the bathroom!"

It started laughing, holding a protuberant belly with its pseudopods. The belly shook like Santa Claus's was supposed to, every bit as red and jellylike, albeit a good deal more noxious. It was like something out of a cartoon. But then lots of stuff here in the Demeter system was. . . . The thing was, it fooled you—things were just as deadly as on Earth. Probably even more so.

"So—there *is* a time element involved," said Matt.

"Oh . . . yeah. Go ahead! Just don't try anything funny—I warn ya! Or—" The thing drew a bladed pseudopod across its neck—and its head tumbled to its feet. The eyes glared up at them. "—else!"

"Sure, sure," said Matt, hurrying his sister and mother along, even as the head crawled back to its body on fibrous tendrils.

They went into the bathroom. Closed the door. The place smelled of mint toothpaste and fragrant bubble bath stuff.

"It's right," said Sally. "We can't get out of here!"

"Shhh!" said Matt, finger to lips. "We've got to talk! Mom, *is* there another way out that we don't know about? Some sort of ejection closet or something."

"No. Just the trapdoor to the next level. And Greenie seems to know all about that."

"We've got to put our heads together on this! We've got to get out of here . . . escape that thing. Dollars to donuts we're like hostages or something. Whoever built those nanites is probably trying to get at Dad through us . . ."

"I've got an idea," said Liz.

". . . but anyway, we just can't stay here and play games with the thing. We've got to think of something and—"

"I fooled with your computer, Matt," said Liz.

"—just *do* something that—"

He did a double take. "What did you say, Liz?"

"I said, I fooled with your computer."

"Liz! I thought I told you to stay out of Matt's things!" said Sally.

Matt held up his hand. "No . . . that's okay, Mom. What did you do to it, Liz . . . and when?"

"Well, after that little stunt you pulled . . . I went out and bought this thing. An automatic override device. I was gonna freak you out with it tomorrow."

"You plugged an override device into my computer!" He grabbed her and Liz cringed. Instead of planting a fist in her face, he planted a kiss. "That's great. Where's the control?"

"In my bedroom."

"I don't know, Matt. That's a reassembled thing out there . . ."

"But it's still my computer. We don't know how much micro and macro redistribution there is . . . And the device . . . It's radio control, right?"

"Oh yeah. Strong, so that it can get through these walls. I made sure of that."

"Never ever let me say anything else derogatory about you, sister dear." He hugged her. "Now, though, all we have to do is to get into that bedroom!"

David Bischoff

Suddenly, an eyestalk sprouted up out of the toilet.

A mouth grew.

"Time's up!" it said.

"What ya want?" said Carbariano. "A nice slice of pepperoni, or what?"

Haldane gawked for a moment. He sputtered.

He was about to run, when Castle grabbed his sleeve.

"What was that old phrase from the twentieth century, Jack? How can you be in two places at once when you're not anywhere at all?"

"Huh?"

"This guy seems to be popping up everywhere," she whispered. "Maybe there's just a lot of guys that look like that security chief here."

"Hey . . . You know, I just fried up a nice bunch of homemade sausage," said the pizza clerk. "How about some of that?"

"You don't want to shoot us or take us somewhere or put concrete galoshes on us?"

"What? All I wanna do is to sell you a couple of slices and some sodas. I'm a humble businessman, with a good product. What more should I be?"

Apparently the guy *wasn't* the mobster Carbariano after all. Just another unusual facet of this most-unusual New York City.

"I'm virtually hungry!" said Haldane. "How about you, Jane."

"I'm not a real pizza person, I'm afraid."

"I've been to Britain. They don't have real pizza there! C'mon, give it a try." Fishing in his pocket, he hauled out the dimes and nickels he'd taken from the bathroom. "Two pepperoni, please."

"Sausage," said Castle. "I'll take sausage."

"Anything to be difficult."

The guy heated up a couple of slices, poured them some Coca-Cola over shaved ice, and then counted out the small amount of money he needed.

They sat at a table out of view of the main window, happy for the respite from the chase and relief from being manacled together. Haldane much preferred being close to Jane Castle under different circumstances—like when it was of her own free will.

"How's your wrist feel?" he said.

"Sore. These glasses aren't the most comfortable thing either."

They ate in silence for a moment.

"This is excellent," she said, washing down a mouthful. "I wonder what it really looks like, though?"

"I take it you're about as thrilled as I am with the questionable reality here."

"All in all, I prefer the flaky dreams that I have, tucked away in my own comfy bed."

"Yeah. Know what you mean."

"No snappy comeback, Haldane? Bed . . . dreams . . . I would think you could milk all kind of sexy innuendo out of that."

"Gimme a break, Castle. I'm a human being, not a wisecrack machine. I just happen to be attracted to you. I'm a male. You're a good-looking and brilliant woman. We share interests. We share a job. We share bathrooms."

She sighed. "Okay, Haldane. You're right."

"Look, we might not get out of this alive. I've been trying to get a date . . . Just a measly date . . . For a long time. I mean, not this . . . Not because you have to . . . Just a chance . . . Uhmm . . . to show you my . . . boring side. . . . Not that there's all that much of it, mind you. I just want to show you that there's a vulnerable part of Jack Haldane."

"Jack, Jack. Look. There's a lot more to life than sexual attraction. There's a lot more to life than . . . well, dating and all the related extravagances. Like work . . . I don't know if you realize this, but I am utterly dedicated to my job."

"I noticed."

"And for good reason. We're on another *world,* Haldane. The first humans . . . We have to work hard, make our places here . . . We don't want to be recorded in galactic history as just a couple of horny Earth people who happened to use Demeter as some cheap twentieth-century drive-in for courting rituals. The future of the human race—the future of *all* races—depends on how well we do our job, how well we integrate and understand the beings on this world, and the ones that pass through it."

"God, you're beautiful when you're serious and virtuous."

"You're just here for a lark, Haldane? They said, go spacewards, young man, and you took the plunge? Come on, wake up, guy. We're in the future, and there's a lot more to life than swapping spit and locking genitals." Her eyes flashed with huge intensity.

He batted his lashes innocently. "But look at the wonderful meaningful things that leads to—a sense of unity, love—a family, companionship. That's still how we're made, biologically, emotionally, psychologically . . . "

"So if I don't fall into your arms, posthaste, you're just going to collapse into a dysfunctional heap."

"You never know."

She sighed. "Jack. You know I'm fond of you. Can't you just leave it at that? For now—"

"Oh, right. Couple years from now, this place will be swarming with bright, handsome young men. Then I'll give it a shot and you'll shrug and say . . . sorry, buster. You had your chance." He grinned impishly. "I just don't want to go down without at least acknowledgment that I tried."

"Okay, you tried . . . and I'm very flattered. Besides, first thing we have to do is to get *out* of this place. I don't know why we're talking about sex and romance. Extended life spans are very helpful for that."

"Just keeping sharp, just keeping our sanity. Just resting." He snapped up the last of the tangy crust. "You're right, though. It would be helpful if we could get out of here. Thoughts?"

"Yes. It's all adding up. This obsession with organized crime of the twentieth century . . . A mock-up of New York City . . . This augmentation to our senses—"

"You bet. Somebody's screwing with our heads!" returned Haldane.

"Exactly. But not just our heads . . . My feeling is that our roles in this are secondary." She took a thoughtful breath. "I think this is a lot about Brogan."

Haldane nodded. "Yeah. I've got the *definite* feeling he's here. So we find him, right?"

"Maybe, maybe not."

"What's that supposed to mean?"

"Whoever is playing with our heads, Haldane, is also playing with Brogan's. We're not together . . . so we may be at cross-purposes. I'd say that if we see him, we should give Brogan a wide berth until we see what his intentions are. . . ."

"This is a *big* city."

"Is it? This really isn't Manhattan. It just looks like Manhattan, Haldane. It's the way we *perceive* it."

"So what can we do about that?"

"The operative word here is 'perceive,'" said the attractive policewoman, tapping the wired-on glasses. "What we have to do now is to find out what this place really is."

"And find Brogan."

"I've got the feeling he's looking for us, Haldane." She chewed on her pizza slice. "And it's not necessarily a *good* feeling, either."

Patrick Brogan, Private Investigator.

Brogan liked the sound of it. It wasn't what he'd chosen in life, and if he had his druthers now, it wouldn't be what he'd be. But he had a gun, now, he had a driver, and he had a sharp suit and an attitude.

He might as well, he realized, run with it.

"Where are we going?" he said, as he got into the front seat with Betty January. He'd forgone the possibility of sitting in the plush backseat of the Rolls Royce she was driving. It simply wasn't his style, this century or his own.

She smelled of a simple but effective flora perfume.

"West Side. They're in a pizza shop. Perhaps if we hurry, we can join them. I'm a *big* pizza fan, Mister Brogan!" she said, pulling out into traffic.

He was about to disabuse her of the notion that there was anything peaceful or convivial about the mission that he'd been sent upon. How much difference would it make, though? She seemed oblivious to just about everything—a studio actress for grade B films, doing her ditzy pretty girl number at the behest of the mad programmers.

"That's good, Betty," he mumbled. "We'll get you some pizza."

"This old boyfriend of mine—every Friday night he'd take me to the bowling alley. We'd bowl tenpins, and eat pizza afterward. A & W root beer, that's what we'd drink. Not real beer. He was a teetotaler. And at the end, he'd kiss me. He wouldn't try anything funny, 'cos he was a regular churchgoer and he had just the best intentions."

"Why didn't you marry him?" said Brogan.

She changed lanes. A puzzled look crossed her face. "I don't know. I honestly don't remember!"

A thought crossed his mind. "Did you go to church, Betty?"

"Me? Oh shuuuurrre."

He leaned toward her. "Betty . . . tell me the truth here . . ."

"Of course, Mister Brogan."

"Have you ever had sex?"

Her eyes opened wide. "Why, Mister Brogan. How could I ever have sex! I'm an android."

"Anatomically correct, though."

"Sure, don't I look that way . . . ? I'm a good girl. I do my job. What, I don't look like a decent kind of girl!" She started snuffling, looking as though she was on the verge of tears. "I was brought up *right*, Mister Brogan."

"The sexy outfits . . ."

"I'm just doing my job. I'm an *actress*. Haven't you figured that out yet?"

He nodded.

This android's being used for blatant sexual purposes seemed unlikely, but even if she had been, it wasn't in her memory banks. She'd been programmed to be a stereotypical sweet, innocent period blonde.

The question was how well she had been programmed—

And what were her gaps?

"Betty, I apologize. You really are a good person, I can tell. I've known that from the beginning."

"Gee, coming from a tough guy like you, that's high praise." She seemed honestly complimented.

"I've got a family, Betty. I've got values. I'm not really a loner private eye. That's just the role that they want me to play."

"Yeah. Well, it's all for fun, right?"

"Their fun. Betty . . . are they listening to us now?"

"Uhmm . . . No, as a matter of fact, not at the moment. There're some other big things going on. But we're probably being recorded."

"Is it possible for you to turn all that off for a while? Just so we can talk, you and I . . . The people with the values!"

"Sure, I have that capability." Her face twitched comically and her shoulders did a little dance. "Okay. On automatic now. No outgoing transmission."

"Betty, you know what they're making me do!"

"Oh, yeah. Go and capture spies. Get the computer crystal. That's the game!"

"They want me to *kill* the spies. And they're not spies, they're my fellow police officers. They're also my friends!"

"Kill your friends! Why would you do that?"

"I don't want to. They've got my family imprisoned. And unless I do what they want me to do here . . ." He paused to choke back emotion. And he didn't have to fake it. "They're going to kill *them*."

"No. They wouldn't do that! This is all just for giggles. It's this big game. And I'm a piece of the game, that's all!"

But her voice sounded doubtful.

Bingo!

He had found the flaw in their programming.

"Betty, I swear I'm not lying. I'm a cop. You know that. I'm for law and order. The people that made you—the man—Dominick Monteleone. He's an old enemy of mine. He's getting his vengeance on me. His vendetta. He's making me suffer . . . He's drawing out my agony."

"But that's not right!" She was incensed.

And that, of course, was the key.

Monteleone had programmed an android, but now he had a real thinking person on his hands . . . And a person whose values and intelligence were independent and derived from less-twisted paths of emotional growth than he had experienced.

They'd created a Virtual babe, a Virtual sweetheart.

The question was, could he get rid of the Virtuality and make it *real*.

"No, it's not. I don't want to kill them. I want to find them, but I don't want to kill them. And it's not a game, kiddo. If I kill them, it's for real."

"It *is*?"

"Yes, I'm afraid so. Now, if you keep the signal off too long, they're going to suspect something. I'm afraid Monteleone and Carbariano are *bad* men. Their games are deadly. I can prove that to you if you'll give me the chance. But at the very least, take me to my friends, help me get that crystal like they want—but don't make me kill them to get it."

"No . . . no, of course not. And you're right, I'd better get the line back on." She did her funny tics and conniptions, and then gave a significant nod. Things were back on-line.

"I don't care how many times you smack me, Mister Brogan. I can't disobey Dominick!"

She gave a "Play along with me" signal.

"That's what a rough private eye is supposed to do, isn't it sweetheart," he said in a bumbling Bogart. "Whack around the dames. I'd push a grapefruit in your face, but there ain't any in the car."

"Okay, just settle down and I'll take you there. But I promise you—Mister Monteleone won't like this at all."

"He can stick it. I'm doin' the job for him and

that's all I'm doin'."

Might as well get in the spirit of the game, he thought.

They took a right-hand turn on Broadway—

And suddenly, they were on Columbus and Eighty-fifth, pulling over by a pizza stand.

"How'd that happen?" said Brogan. And then he remembered that this really wasn't Manhattan. Distance here was Virtual, too.

Inside the pizza parlor was a guy that looked very much like Vinnie Carbariano—but he wasn't.

Brogan bought pizza slices and asked about his quarry.

The pizza man pointed up Columbus.

"They went thataway," he said. "They were looking stuff up in a phone book, and they found some address." He pointed over to the phone booth. "Yeah. Book's still open."

Brogan went to the phone booth.

The book indeed was open.

A large ad caught his eye.

ACME OPTICIAN/OPTOMETRISTS it said.

Ninety-fourth and Columbus was the address.

He touched his own recently added glasses.

Castle and Haldane weren't just waiting around idly.

He hurried to the limo, handed Betty a slice of plain pizza.

"I know where they are," Brogan said.

He went around to his side, but then paused.

He felt someone looking at him.

He looked back at the pizza place.

David Bischoff

The clerk that looked like Vinnie Carbariano was staring at him.

And he held a telephone to his ear.

"We'd better hurry up," said Brogan.

CHAPTER

"Hurry up, will ya?"
said Jack Haldane.

"This is really most irregular," said the optometrist, peering down at the abrupt patient in his chair. Behind him, eye charts hung on the walls. The place had the *de regueur* doctor's office disinfectant smell.

He was a roly-poly fellow in a white smock, with greased-back hair, parted in the middle. He wore Coke-bottle-bottom glasses with thick black frames.

"Yes, well, so is a policewoman like me, pulling a stunt like this," said Jane Castle.

She hit him with a quick jab that sent him sprawling into unconsciousness across Haldane's lap.

"What the hell did you do *that* for!"

"I didn't trust him."

"You didn't trust him!" said Haldane, feeling distinctly uneasy about the whole business.

"No. This is not a normal city. Everyone that's here is here for a reason. Clearly, there being an office like this meant that they expected us to show up. I just wanted to get the scope of this office."

In truth, this notion had occurred to Haldane as well, even as they'd hurried to the office they'd found, and enlisted the immediate aid of this professional. However, he'd been so excited at the notion of getting these bothersome goggles *off* that he'd merely gone along with the first version of the plan.

"So who's going to get these glasses off, then?"

"Who else, Haldane? Yours truly."

"And why not let me get yours off?"

Castle was already eyeing the tools that the doctor had been getting together.

"Because you didn't study forensic medicine in college."

"True." He gulped. "Wait a minute. Forensic medicine studies, like, dead bodies."

"Yes, I've had plenty of experience with dead bodies, Haldane. Now, just lie back and trust me!"

"Oh, why am I not able to conjure up much trust here?" Nonetheless, there was nothing else to do.

He sat back in the chair, pulling the optical equipment around for her.

"You're a good sport, Haldane. The trust is appreciated."

"I hope you say that when we have our first real date."

"Ever think that this may be exactly that . . . And you're passing with flying colors?"

The notion filled him with such bliss that he barely noticed as Castle began fooling around with the miniature screwdriver.

"Still," she said. "Stay very still."

She was leaning over him, and he could smell her, feel her presence close. Despite his tenseness, her nearness comforted him. There was a lot more going on between the two of them, he realized, than simple attraction and banter.

"Excellent," said Castle. "Good fellow, now, if you'll just stay very still here, I'll just take these tiny snippers and—"

What happened next occurred so quickly that Haldane hardly noticed the precise ordering.

However, seemingly, first the door opened.

Then, someone rushed in.

Then lights of a truly kaleidoscopic nature blazed for a brief flashing instant.

And Haldane lost consciousness.

He couldn't have been out for long.

There was a *snap*, as though someone was thrusting a sparkler into his face.

A moment of nothingness.

And he came awake.

He was in a room.

It wasn't the room he'd been in before, brightly

lit and airy, with the smell of disinfectant and magazines on waiting tables. It was a shell of a room, in a haphazard cavern of darkness and shadows, crisscrossed with theatrical skeletal buildings and catwalks, scrims and dim backlighting.

It was as though he was in some cosmic proscenium, with no audience save for God Himself—who might be lowered from the vaulted rafters in the ceiling at any moment to explain what the hell was going on.

Standing in a door without a wall was Patrick Brogan, holding a gun, wearing a set of those glasses. Behind him was that Betty January lady.

There was a movement overhead.

A glimpse of a crane.

The outlines of figures in a seat.

Haldane had the fingernails-on-the-spine feeling of being watched very closely. . . .

Scrutinized from above.

Closer above him was Jane Castle, holding a screwdriver and clippers, peering down through her own glasses, looking frightened and worried.

Haldane's head felt as though he had a spike through his left temple. He reached up to hold his brains in, touched the edge of what were the half-implanted glasses . . .

Snap

The New York City overlay zapped back into place, and again he was in a well-lit optometrist's office.

However, Patrick Brogan was still there, and so was the gun—black and deadly looking.

Pointed at them.

"I'm sorry, Haldane and Castle. I'm going to have to ask for that crystal of yours."

"Lieutenant Brogan," said Castle. "You don't have to aim that at us. What's going on? We were looking for you! And why are you wearing that ridiculous old outfit."

Haldane saw that he was right. In Overlay Reality, Brogan had on a trench coat and a fedora. He looked like a private eye from an old noir movie.

"I think he looks *handsome*," said Betty January.

"Brogan. This isn't totally real," said Haldane.

"I know. They're making me dance their dance, though, Haldane. They've got Sally and the kids." He turned to Castle. "Jane. The crystal. Please."

Held out his hand.

"Sure, Lieutenant." She fished the thing out, tossed it to him.

He caught the thing.

Put it in his pocket.

"What now?"

He had the gun still pointed. "I'm not going to do it." He shook his head. Turned to Betty. "We've got what we need. I can't kill them. I don't care what they do. I can't shoot them."

Snap

Again, the scene for Haldane flipped back to the surreal theater in the cavern.

Only the car attached to the crane hovered closer.

He had the impression of tentacles wiggling from the sooty dark.

Snap

New York again.

"They're just playing games with us, Brogan."

"I know."

"We need to trash the playing board."

"I'll take the crystal back. I have to, or they'll do something to my family."

Haldane walked up to his friend, pain shooting through his head.

He whispered in a low voice. "I take it that this gun is loaded, if you were supposed to kill me."

"Yes. I'm afraid so."

"Give."

Haldane put out his hand.

He could see just a moment of indecision in Brogan's eyes. Then a nod, and a whisper. "Rush me, pal."

Trust. He had to trust his partner. Haldane jumped on Brogan, wrestled the gun from his grasp.

He stepped back, moved the glasses again.

SNAP

The cavern again.

The crane car, hovering.

Quickly, before anyone or anything could possibly stop him, Haldane lifted the gun, switched off the safety and fired three quick shots, straight into the darkness in the car.

The third shot squeezed out a squeak.

Haldane calculated, fired again.

A frenetic squealing.

Whooshings of air from pneumatic controls.

The car wheezed as it flailed about for a moment, then lowered toward them. It looked like an augmented telephone lineman's cubicle, only it hung from the ceiling, apparently from a track.

The car jerked to a stop, swung . . .

And its occupant tumbled out.

"Watch out!" cried Haldane.

Betty January eeeked and stepped aside just in time to avoid the falling body. It came down like a bungee jumper, trailing multiple connections. These snapped off, and the thing plummeted to the floor with a horrible splatting sound.

"Licknose," said Brogan.

"You can see it?"

"Oh yeah."

"And the car."

"Right. It's coming down out of the ceiling."

Haldane was sure that if he put his glasses back fully on, he'd see things exactly that way. However, he just took Brogan's word for it.

Haldane stared down at the fallen creature. It looked like something from the bottom of an alien ocean. The big slugs from the .44 had torn hell out of it. Greenish blood pool. The eyes at the top of stalks were open, but glazed over.

The thing was most certainly dead.

"You knew this guy?" said Haldane.

"Not intimately," said Brogan.

"The puppetmaster of this Virtual Reality," said Castle, pointing at the leads dangling from the crane car, then to the mottled connections into the thing's neural centers.

"Nope," said Brogan. "Real Virtuality. Good job there, Haldane. And Castle—do you think you can get my glasses off too?"

"I don't know, Lieutenant. I may have just lucked out with Haldane. We may not be so lucky with you or me. . . . More brains to burn out."

"Very funny," said Haldane. "But she may be right. Besides, I've got an idea."

He went over to the controls in the car and fired the last of the rounds into them. Sparks flew and gases wheezed.

Something cracked quietly in Haldane's ear, half-attached to the audio portion of the glasses.

"Right. Just short-circuited the whole arrangement. No more Real Virtuality. What you see now is exactly what you get."

Brogan and Castle peered around, blinking.

"Amazing," said Castle. "All a mock-up . . . and yet it seemed so very real."

Betty January jerked. She blinked, looking profoundly troubled.

Then her face went blank—

And reanimated with a nasty grin.

From her purse, she pulled a small gun.

"Very clever," said a voice that wasn't hers. "However, for now, the game still belongs to me."

CHAPTER

All Matt could think
was that it was a good thing he wasn't on the john
when old computer-thing got impatient.

"How did you do that?" Liz demanded, hands on
hips, staring at the rude arrival.

"None of your business. Back out into the living
room, where I can keep the rest of my eyes on you,"
the mouth intoned wetly.

Sally gestured them to obey and Matt nodded.

He knew what was going to have to happen
next. Somehow, he and Liz were going to have
to figure out a way to get back to her bedroom.
Who knew if the automatic controls would work,
but it was something that they were going to
have to try.

He could see in his mom's face that she realized
this, too. Nope, Sally Brogan wasn't the sort to

take things lying down. If there was something that could be done to flummox this thing, you could bet that Sally B. was going to give it the okay. Provided, of course, there wasn't a huge amount of threat to her kids. Now, of course, the threat was a mottled nanotech monster menacing the whole homestead. That wasn't about to go away. To relieve the threat, would, of course, remove the pressure that was on his dad. That would probably free him up a lot.

Besides, Matt thought as he trooped with his family back to the living room, this nano-thing was getting to be a real drag.

It was back in the living room.

Its head crawled out of the toilet, slid along the carpet, and flowed back into the main part of the quivering, wiggly creepie.

"Sit down on the couch, please," said Igor.

They obeyed.

Matt was thinking furiously, but so far the only thing that he was getting was spinning wheels. This thing had problems with them going to the bathroom. How was it ever going to allow them to go off to sister Liz's room?

It was a brain stumper.

"There," it said. "Now, isn't that much more comfortable. Me, I much prefer this room. So much more space to roll about in!" To illustrate, its garish head fell off and rolled around in a geeky, cartoonish dance.

Matt was unimpressed. "You know," he said, "we don't even know your name."

"Name? *Name?* I am the Nameless One!" it said, obviously very pleased with itself.

"That won't do," said Sally. "Nor will 'Legion.' We're clearly stuck in warped conversational mode. We need something to address you by." She turned to Liz. "Darling, why don't you go to your room and get that nice book of names so that we can give our friend here an appropriate one!"

"Okay, Mom." Quickly Liz got up and started running toward her room.

However, an elongated streamerlike thing shot between Liz and the corridor. Liz halted just short of touching it.

"No, no, my dear." A big corrupted-teeth grin dominated the creature's face. "We all stay in here. Unless I give permission to go somewhere." The thick neck spun the head around several times. Jerked to a halt. The tongue wobbled about, then shot out like a huge lasso, enveloping the couch upon which the Brogan family sat. "Just like a big happy group. Shall we play charades then?"

Matt looked at the stuff of the lasso, which was just a few inches from him. It looked solid enough, although most likely it was some kind of combination of force field energy and madly reproducing nanites. This thing would be astonishing if it weren't frightening. And it would be even more scary if it wasn't such a cartoonish ham.

Matt had a thought.

"You're really quite something," he said.

"Why, thank you!" Elephantine ears grew on the side of its head and flapped bashfully.

"I've never seen anything with your stretching abilities. Like, I'd like to go back and get a game to play in my room—but you don't want me to. I wonder if *you* could do it . . ."

"What—like a computer game? How come it's not in my hard drive?"

The thing's torso shot open.

A huge multicolored circuit board emerged, complete and intact.

"Let me see. We've got '*Star Trek*' games, we've got UFO games, we've got Thunderbird games, '*Space: 1999*' games—Geez, you've got all kinds of games in here, kid. What's wrong with one of those?"

"Uhm . . . This is a crystal sim, like you were originally. Too much circuitry and storage for a hard drive."

"Ah. Okay. What's it called?"

"It's called 'Space Precinct.'"

"Cool! Great title, kid."

"It's very popular."

"What's it about?"

"It's about New York cops on an alien planet."

"Brilliant!"

"Great . . . so we can play it?"

The thing shrugged. "Sure, why not. Just tell me which shelf it's on." A pseudopod emerged. Its end was shaped like a hand and in the palm of the hand was an eyeball.

Matt gave Liz a significant look.

A little prod of his knee.

C'mon, Liz. Pick it up here, he thought. *Don't let me have to—*

Liz looked chagrined. "Uh—Big brother. Sorry, but I—uhm—kinda borrowed that game—"

"You *what?*" Matt feigned disgust. "Mom!"

Sally picked up on the deceit immediately. "Liz! Your father and I have told you over and over again . . ."

"Okay, okay! I mean, what difference does it make now? We might not even *live* through this!" said the recalcitrant child.

"That all depends on your old man, kid," said the creature. "Anyway, I can just get it out of *your* room."

"Wow! You mean you can reach *that* far!" said Liz.

"You bet!" It thrust the hand out toward them. The eyeball rolled goofily atop the palm. "And don't you forget it!"

"I won't."

"So describe it to me."

"It's all in my computer console," said Liz. "You know, it's on a desk with casters. You could just roll it out."

"That's good. I'll know what to look for, then." Without further ado, the pseudopod sped off.

"I'm going to like this game, huh?"

"I think so."

"I hope the cops don't always win!"

"Eew!" said Liz. "What kind of game would that be?"

"Me, I prefer games in which green ugly slimy things win!" said Matt.

"Very funny, kid. You know, I'm in this form just

for effect purposes—to register with the fright level of your unconscious. I could change to a Tarn, a Creon—or an earthly matinee idol, if you'd like. . . . But you wouldn't be as intimidated then, now would you?"

"True, very true," said Matt.

"Scared hell out of you before, now didn't I?" the thing chuckled.

"You still do!" said Sally.

"Good. Glad to know it. Now, let me see what we've come up with here!" said the thing. It cranked in its pseudopod. Rolling down the hall, unsteadily but quickly, was Liz's computer, trailing attachments but looking generally intact. "Here we go. This what you're looking for, kids?"

"That's it," said Liz.

"So where is it?"

"It's one of the sims. Do you mind?" said Liz.

She got up.

"Hell no."

"Let me help," said Matt. "Gotta plug it in first."

"Of course," said the thing. "That's something I can deal with." Pseudopods wriggled out, attached the plugs to an outlet. "There you go. Want me to assimilate it? Might be easier."

"Sure, but let's try it this way, first, okay?" said Matt. "Then, when you figure out what's happening, you can swallow it and work it on your own, if you like."

"Whoa. Wait just one nanosecond," said the thing.

Matt's blood froze.

A pseudopod extended out, connected with the side of the computer. This close, Matt fancied he could see the nanites aswarm as the pseudopod changed, blended in with the metal of the computer.

"You're right. It's just a computer," said the thing.

"What'd you think it was—a tank?" said Liz.

"When you're a monster, you can't be too careful about these things. People tend to want to shoot you or blow you up."

"I can't imagine why," said Sally with a grim smile.

"Anyway, it happens in the movies and books on file and the games, of course," said the creature. "So you can't be too careful."

"So you're convinced now I'm not going to pull out an atomic bazooka and blast you?" said Liz, sarcastically.

"Yes. You're going to play 'Space Precinct.' And I have to tell you, I am quite looking forward to it."

Matt nodded to Liz, raising his eyebrows.

Okay, sis. Do your stuff.

"'Space Precinct' . . . right." She turned on the computer, rooted around in a box. She drew out a crystal. Slipped it in. "New York cops on an alien planet."

"I wonder where they got *that* idea," said Sally.

"I'm telling you, it's my absolute favorite game," said Matt.

"I like it a lot, too. Especially the characters. Watch this!"

She hit a few buttons. The screen came on.

Light shot up in a holographic column.

It was a holo of their dad, dressed in his blue uniform.

"Happy Birthday, Liz!" he said.

"Dad," said Liz. "There's a monster in the house!"

And she hit the button that would key in her special program.

                    "Monteleone," said Brogan, stepping back away from the brandished gun.

"Just don't move a step there, people," said the man's voice coming from the blonde with the teased hair and the prominent feminine attributes. "I assure you, these are real bullets here, and they will cut you down just as effectively as the bullets cut down my fallen compatriot." The woman looked down at the alien asprawl in the messy, greenish pools of itself. "I don't know what I'm going to tell his people." He sighed dramatically. "Oh well, I suppose it will be good news to his mother. At least I won't have to kill her now. Too bad . . . He was very good at designing this kind of stuff, don't you think? Real Virtuality . . . A splendid concept, if I do say so myself."

"You know, you look pretty damned funny with big breasts, and wide hips, Monteleone," said Brogan. "Of course, you seem to have retained your rotten attitude."

"Just because your partner had a few lucky shots, suddenly the big man thinks he can finally mouth off. Remember, guy, I've still got your kids, I've still got your wife—and this gun is aimed not just at you, but your precious friends here. Plus, we're still in *my* territory."

"Who *are* you?" said Jane Castle.

Brogan introduced his erstwhile friend and enemy, their current adversary.

"How is that possible?" said Haldane.

"The wonders of nanotechnology," explained Brogan. "Looks like Monteleone not only survived owing to its miracles—he means to throw these little machines into the sands of time, and thus mark out his own name."

"Very cleverly said," Monteleone retorted. "Now, if you'll just come this way, we can end this."

"What if we don't?" said Haldane.

"Well, I'm not going to sit here and *chat*," snapped the ugly voice from the pretty face. "I'll shoot you dead right now. I had hoped to string out the game a little longer . . . watch Brogan suffer, attenuate his suffering. But I'm not going to take any chances with the likes of . . ." He flinched. A tic. Something flickered in his eyes. ". . . y-you."

"You've already taken a lot of chances, Monteleone," said Brogan. "Maybe too many."

"What . . . what . . . are you . . ."

Brogan took a step forward. "Go ahead. . . . Shoot me. Get it over with. Now."

He made no other sudden motion.

He had a hunch. . . .

He just hoped it would pay off. If he could just force the issue.

"Sure. If that's . . w-hat . . . you w-w . . . want," said Monteleone.

His entire face had skewed. Suddenly, Betty January's face was no longer pretty at all. It was twisted, looking as though it were in the midst of some internal struggle.

Which Brogan was counting on.

"You're a killer, Monteleone," he barked. "You're mentally deranged. You're what we're working against in this civilized Universe. You're the reason that cities like Demeter needs cops like us. And the biggest prayer of my life is that one day the Universe won't need us—because it won't have jerks like you!"

The face snarled. "You damned—"

The finger tightened on the gun's trigger.

Haldane looked as though he were about to jump forward, but Brogan lifted a halting hand. "Wait."

The finger tightened no farther.

Instead it relaxed.

"No," said the face, and the voice was Betty January's.

The lips twisted. " . . . this . . . can't . . . happen . . . you're . . . a . . . machine!"

Then the face forcibly moved itself back into its smoother, more attractive role.

The eyes blinked.

And the being that looked out of them was no longer a criminal.

"Golly! You'd think guys like him would learn," said Betty, hands to her head as though to readjust it to the right a turn. "A girl's got her principles." She dropped the gun onto the floor. "I don't kiss on the first date, and I don't kill people!"

"Betty!" said Haldane. "You're back!"

"Gee . . . I could make an exception for a guy like you, Mister Haldane," she said.

"I know," said Castle. "Sometimes I could do that, too!"

"What, kill him?" said Brogan, rubbing some of the tension out of his neck. He then bent over and picked up the gun Betty had dropped.

"No. Kiss him. Thank God I have standards, too."

"Well, I'll do it for you both." Brogan stepped over and planted a wet one on Haldane. "Good shooting there, partner. You saved the day."

"Uhm . . . I'm afraid no amount of Reality doctoring is going to make me enjoy that, Brogan. But thanks for the sentiment."

"I'll take a hug, though!" said Betty.

"You got it, kiddo," said Brogan.

He put his arms around her, and had to admit that for an android she felt entirely real. Even the perfume had a human pheromone kick. She returned the hug humanly and warmly and not without a trace of genuine emotion. In short, the experience was not a bad one at all and he was going to have to consider the possibility that there was a more cerebral seat to the emotions than he'd once believed. . . .

"Thanks, Mister Brogan. I don't suppose the police department could use a good Girl Friday. I think I'm out of a job."

"Assuming we get out of this place alive, Betty."

"I can show you the way out, all right!" she said, gleeful at the news of her reemployment.

"How about this Monteleone guy?" asked Haldane. "He's not going to be real thrilled about our scooting out."

"Too true," said Castle. "I should think we'll have to reckon with him one way or another. And seeing the puissance of his tricks, I suspect that all in all it might be for the best of Demeter City—to say nothing of the civilized Universe—if we faced off with him now."

Brogan turned to Betty January.

"Betty—you think you can help find Dominick Monteleone?"

"Oh suureee—" she said. "He'll be right at the top of the Empire State Building. Just where he said he'd be!"

CHAPTER

22

"What the hell do you think you're doing, kid?" bellowed the creature.

It seemed frozen for a moment, glaring down at its captives, it globular condition for the moment static, its monsterliness at a peak.

Self-doubt for the first time glimmered in its eyes.

"Takes a little while to get this stupid sim going," explained Matt, trepidation tap-dancing on his spine despite the big smile on his face. Something was happening here, but he wasn't sure what—or if it was necessarily good.

The creature looked as though it had swallowed something bad. Like a hand grenade, about to go off.

The holo-sim of Patrick wavered for a moment, flickered—

Then flicked away, like a ghost at the first touch of dawn.

"Matt," said Sally. "Are you sure you have the right sim, dear? We don't want to get Mister Monster upset."

"Damned straight, kid," said the thing. "Listen to your old lady."

"Now wait just a minute," said Sally, standing up. "Menace all you like, but watch your adjectives."

The creature seemed taken aback by this unexpected verbal assault. Interior reverberations seemed to be shaking it as well. For the first time it seemed slightly unsure of itself, even as a control screen began materializing on the monitor of Liz's computer.

Hope stirred in Matt.

Liz kept on tapping away, smiling all the while.

Sally was still standing. Her finger was up, wagging like some deadly weapon. "And 'lady'? That word went out with the early twentieth century. I'm a *woman,* buster, and don't you forget it!"

For a moment, the monster seemed cowed. Its greenish, spotted skin moiled, pseudopods all withdrawn, protuberant eyes agoggle.

Feeling the power of her oratory overtake her, Sally took a confident step forward.

"You know, when I came here, I was hoping to find a new Universe with a new consciousness. But you know what? It's just the same old male Saturday afternoon drivel. Are you listening to me, whoever you are behind that silly, fright mask facade! Can't you think of anything more original than power and domination for goodness' sake!"

That seemed to be entirely to much for the creature to take. Its sides expanded, blowing up balloonlike and its eyes seemed to pop from whatever it was using for a skull.

"This is too much for me to take. I must kill one. Only one will do the plan no harm!"

It stalked toward Sally.

She stood her ground.

She took off her belt.

"Okay, you bastard. Come and get me. Kill me if you like, but you're not going to get me to scream anymore."

For his own part, Matt was just as happy not to be the object of her rage. Her eyes, her very being seemed to radiate total fury.

Alas, the monster didn't seem terribly fazed.

Two pseudopods grew, becoming hands. The hands streamed toward Sally Brogan, warty things that looked especially created for throttling.

Say what you like, whoever was the intelligence behind this thing was about as subtle as turds in a punch bowl.

"Liz . . ." said Matt.

"Okay, okay, I'm getting it," said his sister.

"Maybe you'd better let me . . ."

"No way. You'll foul things up for sure," she answered. "Let me tell you, bub. You're not the only computer whiz in this house!"

She tapped another sequence.

Code raced along the screen.

"Yes!" she cried.

The creature's hands wrapped around Sally's neck. She flailed away gamely at it with her belt, with alarming yet wholly inadequate energy.

"No," said Matt.

"Urk," said the thing.

The manic thyroid eyes in its head suddenly went strabismic, twirling about in a conniption dance.

The thing loosed its stranglehold on his Matt's mom, withdrew like rubber bands snapping back into its roly-poly self.

"What's happening?" Matt asked Liz.

"I'm not sure," she said. "Whatever it is, it seems to be working."

The protruding oculars stopped twirling.

They focused on the two behind the computer bench.

"You!"

A hand streamed out, this time holding a large scimitar, gleaming and intensely sharp.

"So much for keeping you alive!" it said.

The weapon began to swipe their way.

"Liz!" said Matt.

Desperately, his sister rattled off another command.

The scimitar-limb halted as though it had struck some kind of wall of force.

The creature looked totally baffled.

"Hey," it said. "This isn't—"

Liz hit another button, and the creature's limb retracted so quickly that it accidently lopped off the protruding eyes.

They bounced onto the floor like a couple of tennis balls loosed from a court.

They stared up from the floor for a moment in total bemusement . . .

And then they grew legs, scurried back to be absorbed into the greater mass . . .

Boink

Instead, they bounced off, rolled back.

They wobbled for a moment, looking as baffled and frustrated as a pair of monster's eyeballs could possibly be.

Matt looked over to the computer's monitor. A graphic had formed, a three-dimensional portrayal of the creature's present shape.

"Whatever it seems to be," said Liz, quietly, "it's still just a machine . . . and it's got your computer enmeshed . . . all the nanites have what amounts to your computer's sorta-DNA pattern . . . and that's what's controlling the nanite flow."

"And now we're controlling my computer?"

"Yeah," said Liz. She took a deep breath. "Question is now, what do we *do* with it?"

"Well, first things first," said Matt.

"You've got a suggestion."

"You bet. How about DELETE?"

Liz looked at him and smiled.

"I think we can manage that."

David Bischoff

She was about to punch the ERASE sequence, when he stopped her.

"Wait a minute," Matt said, smiling slyly. "I think I've got a better idea."

The Empire State

Building was about thirty-feet high.

Or what passed for the Empire State Building, anyway.

More like about two sections of the Empire State Building, actually, thought Patrick Brogan as he hurried after Betty January, guiding them to downtown.

Without the power of the Real Virtuality glasses, Monteleone's New York looked quite a bit different.

They'd taken the Rolls Royce—but it turned out to be not a Rolls Royce at all, but rather a car with a seat and bare metal covering, more golf cart than Rolls. The entire ride had been a chiaroscuro of artifice, figurative papier-mâché skeletons upon which to hang and structure an artificial reality that nonetheless had a kind of solidity, a feel. Again, a good deal of the West Side had been bypassed in a snap. They'd rolled down Broadway quickly, then parked just short of their destination, so as not to alert too quickly the creator of this world as to their arrival.

"You sure we don't want to just split this place . . . Come back with Podly and about a zillion troops?" asked Haldane.

"No. Most emphatically, we must get him now . . ." said Brogan. "He's still in control anyway. He could very well attack us from the rear on the way out. This way, we at least get to face him. And we have an ally here to help us. Right, Betty?"

"Well, I guess there's nothing I can do but do my best! I mean, now that I've switched sides!" She shook her head sorrowfully. "I would never have worked for that fink if I'd known that what he was after was universal domination! I thought it was just all a fun game. Sheesh!"

"A blow struck for liberation, Betty," said Jane Castle. "It will be good to have you working with us."

"Gollleeee . . . Just imagine . . . Me, miles and miles above the surface—a precinct house . . . Who ever would have thought."

"Believe me, when I went to Police Academy, Betty," said Brogan. "This was about the last thing on my mind."

"Tell me about it," agreed Haldane. "I'll never look at the Empire State Building the same again. . . ." He shook his head and shrugged. "My big question is . . ." He gestured all about him at this bizarre mock-up of Manhattan. "Why a place that literally looks like that famous Steinberg *New Yorker* cover of the Universe according to New Yorkers?"

"Working something out psychologically?" suggested Castle.

"Exactly," said Brogan. "Isn't that what we all do in our own way in our lives. . . . Only Monteleone had a pretty warped background . . . and he's working it out on a very grand scale."

"And he wanted you to help," said Castle.

"I've heard that revenge is a dish best served cold," said Brogan. "That's clearly Monteleone's philosophy. The difference is that he wants his with his own peculiar seasonings."

They reached the entrance. The doors were open. No one barred their passage.

The went in and found themselves faced with elevators.

"I'd feel a lot better with the stairs," said Castle. "Is that possible?"

"Sure," said Betty January. She pointed to a sign that said EXIT in large red letters. "That's the way to go!"

They followed her, ready for anything.

"Why here?" asked Haldane, even as he stayed alert, his gun out and ready.

"Monteleone was always fascinated with the Empire State Building," Brogan remembered aloud. "He felt as though it was some kind of time machine. I remember once when we were in college we went up to the observation deck and he said, 'You know, it's not just Greater New York and New Jersey that you can see from here, Patrick. It's the past.' From this construct around us, I'd say that there's absolutely no doubt that the man is fascinated with his own particular, skewed version of the past. . . . Why, exactly, you'd have to ask his analyst."

"It's the base of operations for the underworld down here," said Betty, matter-of-factly. "And also for the other controlled operations above."

"What, like Mrax Computers?"

Betty January shook her head. "Partially. This is the place where he controls the nano-whatsits!"

"Excellent!" said Brogan. "This is where he'd be, of course. It's the center of things."

"Could be the deadliest as well," said Castle.

"And it's also the point where we have the biggest hope of calling out for any help we can get from Podly," said Brogan.

"Yeah. You'd think he'd be storming this place by now," said Haldane.

"Maybe he can't . . ." said Castle.

"It seems like we've been down here a while, but we probably haven't. Podly can't get a reading on us! He just plain doesn't know where we are, that's all," said Brogan.

"And you're saying that what we need is a call out?" said Haldane. "You should have told me. Could have used one of those phone booths downstairs."

"Unlikely. If there are any communications lines, they're going to be upstairs."

At the top of the stairway was a door.

Brogan lifted his gun.

"Ready, people?" he said, raising his gun head, getting the feel and touch and balance of it.

"No," said Haldane. "But this is where's it's happening. Let's do it!"

They pushed open the door and, armed only with guns, determination, and wits, stepped into the control room of some future hell.

CHAPTER

When Patrick Brogan
had been a child, growing up in Brooklyn, his
Uncle Shaunnessy had taken him deep into an old
section of Flatbush, to one of the last Curiosity
Shoppes that existed in the Greater New York
area. This was after the turn of the century, of
course, and modernity and progress were the sub-
jects most on everyone's minds. There wasn't much
room for antiquarianism, so Shannon's Odds and
Ends was one of the last of its breed. Although it
had some, Shannon's was not an antique shop per
se. Rather, it dealt in effluvia of former ages. Old
books and magazines, photographs, music sheets.
Magazines and buttons, shoelaces and bow ties.
Patrick had particularly delighted in the old but
still-working toys. Ingenious tops and yo-yos, and
balls and jacks and other oddments of bygone days.

The shop had smelled not just of dust, but of old wax and exotic perfumes, of ideas and realities that had a much different feel than today. It was like a window into the past, and yet at the same time a crypt. It was like Miss Haversham's wedding cake in Charles Dickens's *Great Expectations*, a towering crumbling monument to days that would never be seen again.

As he walked into the central command control of Nicholas Monteleone's Old New York, he felt as though he were walking into some hidden back room of that Olde Curiosity Shoppe. The Italian Immigrant Room. A cleaned-up, less-dusty version of that nonexistent room, perhaps—but the principle and contents were here.

The first thing you noticed were the pictures. They hung on the walls in beautiful, ornate early twentieth- and nineteenth-century frames. There were portraitures and sepia daguerreotypes. There were tintypes and blown-up movie frames. They showed women and men, posing by cars or shops with various names of businesses. They showed weddings and funerals and family portraits of men with handlebar mustaches and women who looked frightened and trapped. They all seemed to have dark eyes and dark complexions, often with Roman noses or Sicilian chins.

The children looked like children of Now, lost and imprisoned in Then, with stiff, haunted expressions.

The shelves were stacked with books, and the room was filled with expensive old furniture. An old gramophone sat in the corner. Enrico Caruso tenored an Italian aria from it. Dolls and toys and knickknacks sat helter-skelter everywhere, beside candelabra and musical instruments. A faded concertina oozed toward the gramophone, looking as though it were pining to play with the Great Caruso.

On the sideboard was an old-fashioned espresso machine, along with cups and spoons and an ancient china sugar bowl.

It smelled of furniture polish and strong coffee, with just a sweet background of barbershop talcum and potent cheap cologne. Hovering beside all this was the taste of madness and determination, as though from some decaying pasta with Mussolini sauce.

"Oh my God," said Castle. "Curiouser and curiouser."

"Where is he?" said Haldane.

Betty January pointed to a huge mirror on the far wall, framed in raised Venetian curlicues. "Behind there."

"Monteleone!" cried Brogan. "It's time to talk. You haven't got us hooked up now to your infernal devices. We're free of your games now! And there's no reason we can't bargain!"

A voice seemed to undulate from the wall. "Isn't there, Patrick? I have your family. You still dwell in my domain. How do you know there isn't an army of gangsters out there, even now, loading up their tommy guns, hmm? And how do you know I don't have other tricks up my sleeve?"

David Bischoff

"Oh, I'm sure you do, Dominick. And I'm sure this vendetta of yours is keen on your mind. But listen—what you've accomplished—why, it's incredible. The levels of technology you've scaled . . . The things of which you are capable with these tiny programmed machines . . . Why, it could make the universe a better place. Why waste yourself on a criminality of the past? Why give yourself to obsession? You have power, yes . . . Power now, and perhaps power in the future. Good can come out of evil. . . . Think of it!"

The reflectivity of the mirror began to alter. Swirling currents of patterns coalesced, faded, became translucent. The glass began to bow outward, like something out of a glassblower's pipe.

A scene began to form, a vision like something inside a milky, misty crystal ball in the hands of a demonic high-tech wizard.

Dominick Monteleone.

He wore a suit and a tie and well-polished shoes.

The crime lord sat within this sphere of crystal, a gangster Merlin, holding a wand of controls. Wires snaked out from implants in his head, an array of leads connected to heaving, plastiorganic consoles.

"*Bono sera.* Do not bother to try and use the *caldos* on me. Do not be a *finnoch*. My shield here is impermeable to bullets, rays, bricks, and bats," said the voice.

"I hope you don't mind if we hang on to them," said Brogan.

"If it gives you the illusion of security—by all

means," said Monteleone, a mild smile on his face. His eyes were milky and glazed. He looked as though one of the wires were leaking drugs directly into his brain.

"What do you say, Dominick?" said Brogan. "There's still hope for you."

The glazed eyes turned toward Betty January. "Ah—Betty. You are now the successful result of an experiment. A truly sentient machine—developing a conscience and moral mobility independent of orders. Betraying the boss, yes!" A wry, dry chuckle. "What do you have to say for yourself?"

"All I gotta say is I did what I had to do, Mister Monteleone. Kill me if you want to. . . . But don't forget . . . There must be some of the ethics and morals in you that you put into me. . . . Gee . . ." Chomp of gum. "*Somewhere!*"

"The lady's got a definite point," said Haldane.

"Perhaps you might search your soul," suggested Castle sympathetically.

"That's true. *Very* true, Dominick!" echoed Brogan, remembering the way his former friend had been. "We used to talk about that in college! Right and wrong, Dominick! But not just out of moral codes . . . But for the greater good. . . . You used to be so idealistic. You wanted the best for everyone."

"Until *nobody* wanted the best for me," murmured Monteleone. "Except for my family. They alone believed in me. . . . Believed in my visions."

"Only because they were dying—spiritually and politically. All this"—Brogan gestured around

him—" it's just the memorabilia and sentimental-
ity of a past of killers and thugs and moral imbe-
ciles, chained to a way of life they hadn't thought
out, locked into their own limited language of life.
This is no foundation to build any kind of future
on. Not only because it's sick . . . Because it won't
work. History created your family, perhaps. But
there's no future in it!"

The eyes cleared somewhat, stared down at him
with fury.

"History created you. And there's no future for
you."

"There's always a future for what I . . . *we* . . .
do, Monteleone," said Brogan, pointing toward his
companions. "Because we don't do it because we're
programmed to do it. We do it because we want a
good life for ourselves . . . and a good life for others.
If the Universe didn't need cops, we wouldn't be
cops. But every single one of us would be in a job
that would help others."

"Absolutely," said Castle.

"Yeah," said Haldane, fight and school spirit
shining in his eyes. "Go team!"

Brogan could have done without the pep rally
from his partner, but the intensity of his own seri-
ousness carried him over being irked.
Monteleone's abandonment of ethics and morals
to return to a life of crime for the sake of scientific
research was as much a warped psychological
need for the comfort and security of family and
power and riches as it was—for practical mone-
tary backing. He well knew the whole time that a

partial factor in the man's descent had been a series of failed personal relationships. Brogan had always felt that perhaps his relationship with Monteleone was one of the relationships that had failed, and he'd never known it because *he'd* been at fault. He'd let his college buddy down. Of course, he'd been young and self-absorbed. Who could have seen it coming? Nonetheless, when he heard that the man was involved with the Mafia again, Brogan felt guilty. Doing his job, trying to destroy the crime ring and, finally, shooting and killing Monteleone did not exactly assuage his guilt.

If he could only appeal to that shred of the old Monteleone that was there, Brogan felt there might yet be hope for a renewal, a change.

At any rate, he had to try.

"Please," he said. "Nick. I'm sorry I let you down, and I'm sorry . . . I'm sorry I shot you. I was doing my job. Is there any way you can use your nanites to repair the damage in your heart . . . Is there any way they can eat away the cancer that's grown in your brain?"

"My head's just fine, Patrick," said the voice. "And my heart? Well, let's just say it works much better than the old one." He swiveled a little bit, stared down at them from his high-tech perch. "Now then. Far be it from me to be discourteous and a poor host. Please, help yourself to refreshments. Have a seat. There are things we must talk about. Cabbages. Kings. . . . "

Talk.

His first reaction to the notion was to say no.

But time was something they had to buy, Brogan knew.

With time, there was hope for his family, hope for them. Because Castle and Haldane were right. Podly and company were out there. Out there, somewhere . . . And that particular Creon was not exactly good at waiting. Without them returning on time, he'd find some way to come after them, Demeter City regulations be damned. Podly was far more interested in the spirit than the letter of the law.

He turned to the others, nodded.

"I think we could do that. With time, there is the possibility that I can talk some sense into the guy," said Brogan.

"I thought you already had a heart-to-ice cube with the guy—at which point you went out to hunt us down," Haldane reminded him.

"I achieved that particular goal. Now on to the next." Brogan turned to Castle. "Why don't you go ahead and hand over that crystal. I don't think it's any good to us at this point."

"Excellent. How clever," Monteleone responded immediately. "Appease me. I enjoy appeasement. Please—just place it on the table there, by the coffee urn, Ms. Castle. And then, by all means, help yourself. It's very late in your shift by now, in all senses of the word, and I'm sure you could use a little lift."

Castle stepped forward and put the crystal where she had been instructed to.

A hole sphinctered in the table, swallowing the

crystal up with a distinct gulping sound.

"Well, so much for the purpose of our visit," said Haldane, disgustedly. "Now we've got nothing to prove anything."

"How about a nice coffee bean buzz?" suggested Castle. "Come on, Haldane. I'll pour you a demi-tasse."

"Lots of sugar, please."

Brogan asked for his straight. Betty January demurred, simply taking a seat and looking profoundly interested in everything, big eyes taking the whole scene in as though seeing and hearing such marvelous events for the very first time.

Brogan took his and sat down in a high-backed chair. He took a bitter sip. He found his head clearing a bit. Nothing even near to Virtual about this coffee—it was strong and black with a strong kick.

Even so, sitting in the middle of this odd Italianate junque shop, sipping espresso and talking to a madman pulled from the grave by microscopically tiny machines, had the definite feeling not of Real Virtuality, nor Virtual Reality, but absolute *surreality*.

"There. Feel a little better now?" asked the man behind the glass bulb.

"Excellent espresso," said Castle.

"Yeah. Smooth. I could use a donut, though," said Haldane.

A chuckle. "I always suspected that all cops majored in donuts 101 at the Police Academy. Mister Haldane, you'll find some chocolate biscotti right behind the machine. Please indulge."

Haldane stepped over, pulled a glass container out from behind the silver machine. "Oh yeah. Thanks." He offered them around. Only Castle took one.

"You'll be happy to know that I have a direct espresso drip in one of these wires . . . so in fact, I am being sociable, I am joining you."

"Good to know," said Brogan.

Talk, talk, talk, Nick.

The more you talk, the better chance we've got.

"Yes. Really, perhaps this is all just as well—I am sorry about Licknose, but clearly his efforts did not anticipate the ingenuity of our gamesters. Ah well, I know for sure that you are suffering. True, Patrick?"

"You have to know I'm suffering, Nick. You've got my family, and they're in real jeopardy."

"Oh yes, indeed they are. Although I shall let up on you a bit here, and let you know that no harm has come to them," said the Nano-King. "Merely playing games. I have been developing interesting sentient AI using my nanites, you see. Merely a matter of synchronizing colonies of them to function . . . well, to function as AI computers do. Presently, an AI is still watching over your crew most effectively—an AI controlled, of course, by my larger AI nano-colony controls here . . . I must say, putting them through the ropes up there . . . and putting you people through the games makes me realize that I don't have to kill you to get my vendetta accomplished."

Brogan raised an eyebrow. "I wish I could say

that sounds like good news. What makes me think there's something about the altered plan that I'm not going to like?"

"Let me fill you in on a little background, before I reveal your fates," said Monteleone. "You see, far from being old and out of date, the Sicilian method of power and control is ancient and wise, and knowledgeable about the very stuff of human nature. I have studied it deeply, and I have decided that this is the way that the known Universe must be run. And it is not just the need for power or revenge here that drives me—but a sense of the destiny of intelligent beings . . . the course of the natural evolution of intelligence."

"Super Mafia as overlords?" said Haldane. "Why am I not excited?"

"Please. Hear me out. There are ways I can silence you that will not be pleasant," growled the would-be Don Monteleone.

"Sorry about my partner. He can't help but state bald truth. But go ahead, Nick. Let's hear this vaunted plan of yours."

"You see, the wonderful thing about nanites is that they reproduce themselves so very quickly. And they can be programmed so exquisitely . . . from far distances. A case in point—the nanite I smuggled into your house, Brogan, using that test market sim for Junior's computer. Similar tricks can be used to spread my nanites around the known Universe. Add matter and *voilà*! Artificial Intelligences, programmed for conquest . . . programmed to be under my control. Just think,

Brogan. I won't simply be a Godfather of this particular Mafia family. I will be the Deity Father— of the known Universe. I will bring forth the ideas and traditions of my people—into the twenty-first century . . . and far beyond."

"Pardon *my* big mouth," said Jane Castle. "But this doesn't sound like a Mafia complex. It's a bit more like a Napoleonic complex, don't you think? Perhaps some psychoanalytic nanite colony device might be more suitable . . . and perhaps you'd be the first candidate for its couch."

"I hope you don't think that any thinking government or being is going to stand around and allow that to happen, Monteleone," said Brogan.

"Please, let me finish. You really are quite a boisterous bunch, for your lack of power here. Are you going to allow me to have my time to do my dramatic plan—or shall I just get very perturbed, kill you and your friends, and kill your family and be done with it. Hmm?"

"You're right," said Brogan. "We'll keep our mouths shut unless asked questions. Right, guys?"

Castle and Haldane nodded penitently.

"Mind if I chew gum?" said Betty January. "My mouth comes open sometimes when I chew gum."

"Of course you can chew gum with your mouth open, Betty," said Monteleone. "You wouldn't be you if you didn't do that."

"Gee, thanks, Mister M. You know, you got some good stuff in you. You really ought to consider not thinking about universal domination and just open a pizza parlor or somethin'."

"Monteleone's Nano-Pizza!' said Haldane.—Yeah! I'd invest. You guys make the best."

A door opened.

Vinnie Carbariano stepped in.

In his hands was a particularly large and vicious-looking tommy gun, cocked and ready to let loose a hail of death.

"Sorry," said Haldane.

"I truly appreciate your praise," said Monteleone. "But as you may recall . . . I have the floor."

"I'd put dose guns down too, if I were you," said Carbariano. "Dey make me kinda noivous."

They obeyed.

Brogan somehow felt more naked now. However, he'd put his on the ornate coffee table in front of him, within easy reach if necessary. Carbariano didn't seem to mind the guns being around as long as they weren't in their hands.

"Now then. As for Mob domination of the Universe . . . A very real future, I think. You see, we've been perfecting a curious and different brand of nanite colonies. I've been experimenting with them in the colony that's kept your family so well occupied. You see, I very well realize, Brogan, that governments, alien and human, are not going to want to go along with domination by thugs who look like Carbariano."

"Hey!" said the mobster.

"Sorry, Vinnie. You've got an important place in my scheme of things, but you're simply not always going to look like you do now."

"Oh well."

"Exactly. As I was saying, Brogan . . . With these nanites, domination will not be from without . . . but from within . . ."

A lower door of the espresso maker opened.

A small blob of black, roiling stuff leaked out, collected into a ball, and then plopped onto the floor.

As Brogan watched, three more blobs poured from the machines, rolled forward, each taking a different path.

One rolled toward Betty, one toward Haldane, one toward Castle . . .

And the largest, nastiest one rolled toward Brogan.

"The wonders of nano-technology extend from the micro to the macro," explained Dominick Monteleone. "And then back to the micro."

Brogan stared at the blob that rolled toward him.

As it neared him, he could see that it wasn't organic, as he'd thought at first. Rather it was a globular formation of shifting gray mass, constantly changing, working in some kind of organizational progression beyond his ability to conceive.

It was like something out of a Virtual Reality computer, come to life . . .

. . . and crawling toward him.

"No way that thing is touching me!" said Haldane, standing up out of his chair.

The response of his assigned blob was immediate.

A tentacle darted out, wrapped around Haldane's legs, and pulled them out from under him.

He went back into his chair, butt first.

"Please don't move. It will make everything all that much more difficult," said Monteleone. "You see, what you see crawling toward you are nothing less than your new brains . . . nanite brains . . . controlled by my computers."

A sordid smile crossed Monteleone's thin lips.

"I just want you to know that, Patrick," he said, in a softer voice. "I just want you to know that what will be running your body in the future won't be you—it will be me. You'll be my flunky from now on, Patrick. You and your colleagues here. You and your family. You'll be imprisoned in your own brain, powerless . . . Watching as you do things, say things, that serve my purposes and my purposes only."

The gray roiling blob progressed closer. It extended two pseudopods, like antennae questing for scents, for signals of prey.

Suddenly one of them extended quickly, wrapping around Brogan's ankle. Alarm shot up his spine. *Do not panic*, he told himself. *Don't do anything that will allow you to lose control. Mental control is the only hope here.* He had to figure out what to do. . . . There must be something possible. . . .

His mind raced.

"We've already prepared the mode of entrance," said Monteleone. His snakelike fingers danced over controls. The glasses that the police all wore now popped fully off, falling onto their laps.

Leaving metal-rimmed jack holes in their skulls.

"You see, the material of the nanite colonies need but to thin itself to a thread mere molecules thick and slip along your neural pathways. Directly into the cerebrum, the cerebellum—through your control centers, in short.

"Except, of course, for Betty. We've sent out a different program for her control center. Looks as though we'll just have to get rid of a few malfunctioning ethical centers in you, dear."

"Yeah," said Carbariano. "And, Boss . . . could you make her a little looser about her, like . . . sexual mores this time!" The thug grinned lasciviously.

Betty twisted her face at him. "Yeah, but even so I'll have enough taste not to use them on you!"

Brogan stared down at the thing crawling toward him. Both Castle and Haldane were looking toward him with "What do we do now" looks.

A pseudopod extended and wrapped around Brogan's legs.

The main part of the body pulled itself up to his legs, wrapped itself around his legs, and began crawling upward, like some psychotic slug headed toward a bloody meal.

"Monteleone . . ." said Brogan. "Dominick . . . This won't make you happy. All the power in the Universe won't make you happy. That's not what it's about. Can't you see that?"

"No, I'm afraid not, Patrick. All I can see is a brilliant man, shunned and denigrated by his peers, who had to go home for what he needed. And when he did what he had to do, his college buddy came and sought him out and shot him down. That's the truth, call it what you like. . . . This is my revenge, Patrick. . . . And I'm going to enjoy it for a very, very long time. . . . Think about this, Patrick. My nanites will be able to repair your body for years to come. I'm going to be able to keep you alive for a very long time. You'll be able to see just how wrong you are about my plans . . . because you'll be able to literally witness them come to full fruition."

The thing was heavier than it looked.

It wiggled up into Brogan's lap.

It made tentative movement farther upward with coiling pseudopods, twining into a single narrow thread.

A glance toward his companions told Brogan that the same thing was happening to them. They only had a matter of seconds before these narrow threads found their way to the jacks . . .

. . . penetrated.

And then they were doomed to be the pawns of this madman . . .

"No!" he said.

He made to push the thing away.

The blob reacted immediately, wrapping two strong pseudopods around his waist and the chair. He couldn't move.

Monteleone laughed. "I knew you'd break, Brogan. I knew you wouldn't be able to take it."

The cold baiting voice steeled his nerves. He stopped struggling, and turned implacably toward Monteleone. "Go ahead, Nick. Stick all you like into my head—but you'll never truly be sure I'm really your slave . . . I promise you that."

A thread of stuff, shining in the light, slid up toward the jack.

Stopped.

Suddenly it withdrew.

Surprised, Brogan looked over to the others. Their blobs were descending as well, undulating down their bodies like pieces cut out of some other Reality and pasted on this one.

They slithered down thusly, hit the floor, drew together into one large version of their previous self. Then together, they flowed toward the espresso machine.

Monteleone was clearly not happy with their actions. His fingers played frantically over a keyboard. He blinked rapidly as he stared down at the machine.

"No. No, what are you doing!"

What *were* the roiling nanites doing? wondered Brogan.

Going for a cuppa?

As they watched, the blob covered first the table, then the coffee urn.

Quickly it seemed to bore into the thing, absorbing, reworking.

The sound was a strange combination of the scream of attacked molecules and the whir of shifting energy.

The coffee urn quickly and totally disappeared into the nanite collection. The resultant new mass turned a silvery color then grew protuberances.

Eyes jutted out bizarrely.

A great big loony mouth opened.

In the torso was what looked like the mass of a rearranged home computer.

The eyes rolled wildly. The lolling tongue wagged.

"Hey, gang!" said the monster. "Let's party!"

CHAPTER

Brogan watched,
astonished, as Monteleone desperately jabbed at
his controls.

Carbariano had an entirely different reaction to
this new and unexpected arrival.

He leveled his tommy gun and started pumping
loud lead into its body.

"Hey!" said the creature, frowning. "That's not
at all what I had in mind!"

It whipped a new, metallic pseudopod out,
lashing it around the dark-suited mobster's gun.
With great force, it hurled it against Monteleone's
bubble-capsule, smashing the gun into pieces.

Haldane wasted no time. He hurled himself
against the mobster, knocking him back against
the wall. His fists flew with both skill and released
anger and frustration.

Fortunately, this seemed to be the principal version of Carbariano. He was Creon flesh and whatever, and though he was large and put up a fight, within moments he was on the ground, bloody-nosed and down for the count. Haldane's pugilistic skill, pushed no doubt by frustration and anger, had won the moment.

Taking his opportunity, Brogan scooped his gun up off the table. He wasn't looking a gift opportunity in the mouth. He ran over to Betty.

"Is there a way up to that capsule entrance?" he asked.

However, before she could answer, a loud drilling sound filled the room.

Brogan looked up.

"That thing," said Castle, pointing toward the goofy monster. "It's trying to get into Monteleone's capsule!"

The nano-colony creature's pseudopod had formed a large buzz saw–like object that was twirling and clawing at the bulletproof castle. Great whirls of matter were being shaved off.

The thing was getting in!

The capsule cracked. The creature pulled the bubblestuff away. Inside, Monteleone retreated, still trying to override the nano-controls.

Suddenly, there was an electrical arc around the nano-colony creature. Sparks jumped from its computer parts. Shaking, it turned around toward Brogan.

"Can't control this any longer," said a voice that Brogan recognized as his son Matt's.

"We're okay, Dad!" said the voice of Liz. "We love you. Good luck!"

Then the thing's shape started crumbling in upon itself. Soon it looked like a melting snowman—

. . . dwindling . . .

And then it was just a bumpy puddle of metallic-sheened junk upon the floor.

Brogan wasn't entirely sure what had happened, but he wasn't going to wait around and analyze.

He stepped over for a clear shot at his adversary in the cracked capsule, drew a bead.

"You're under arrest, Monteleone. Get out of that thing and come down here."

"I'll be damned first!" cried the man, and brought up his own gun, and fired. The bullet thundered past Brogan's ear and thumped into a high-backed chair. Brogan ducked behind another chair, then peeked up over it.

The attachments to Monteleone's head were popping off. A door behind the man irised open. He fired a few more rounds through the hole in the capsule, and then clambered out.

"Betty," said Brogan, "where is he going?"

"Only way out other than past this room is through the observation area and down a ladder," said the blond android.

"That's where I'm going. Haldane—down the other way. We've got to capture him before he escapes!"

"Gotcha."

Haldane grabbed up mobster Carbariano's gun, pulled open the door, and headed out.

"You two stay here, in case he comes back!" said Brogan.

"Right!" said Castle.

Brogan stormed through the door and up a series of stairs, banging through all the doors that read OBSERVATION FLOOR.

He was already puffing hard when he reached the top, but desperation and determination drove him on. He pushed through the final door . . .

And found himself "outside."

Some sort of interior fog had moved in. Restless searchlights played in the distance. It smelled of the cold sea out here, and Brogan fancied he heard the sound of traffic, far far below. . . . A wind swirled the fog. Even though he knew that this was a fake Empire State Building, every impression here was of something real—and very high up off city streets.

His eyes adjusting to the darkness, he turreted around.

A sound of footsteps.

Hands and feet mounting a metal ladder.

A light swirled through the fog, and he saw a figure climbing up a ladder against the fence bordering the edge of the building.

"Monteleone! Stop! Or I'll shoot!" Brogan cried, stepping forward.

He raised his gun toward the figure.

The man reached the top of the fence. Monteleone turned around. His cold eyes looked down on Brogan.

"It won't be the first time, Brogan. And probably won't be the last. . . ."

Monteleone brought his own gun around.

The muzzle spoke.

A flash of flame shot out.

The bullet missed, ricocheting off.

Brogan jumped, ducked, whirled, and came up blasting.

The first bullet pinged off metal.

But the second and third slapped directly into Monteleone's chest.

Monteleone put his hands on his wounds, looked down at Brogan. "You got me, pal." He shook his head, smiling. "Is this the end of Dominick Monteleone?" The smile became a sinister grin. "Naw! *Va fangula,* Brogan." He tilted back, looking over the edge. "Top of the world, Ma!"

And then he tumbled off over the side.

He did not scream on the way down.

And so, thought Brogan glumly, *history repeats itself yet again.*

Brogan scampered up the ladder and peered down to make sure his foe indeed had fallen, that there were no tricks here—

He looked down.

The body of Dominick Monteleone was lying on a concrete floor, spread-eagled and still.

Brogan hurried down the ladder, then hurled open the door and ran down the steps of the pseudo–Empire State Building.

Outside, in half-real, backstage land, he turned around the edge of the building.

Haldane was bending over the body of the fallen crime lord.

"You okay, Brogan?"

"Yeah. I'm okay."

"Good. You'd better come here and take a look at this, then."

Trepidation filling him, Brogan went to Haldane's side.

The body still had the same position, and indeed it was as lifeless as it had looked from the top of the faux–observation tower.

However, Brogan immediately saw what Haldane meant.

The top of the skull was off, hanging by a hinge.

Inside, the entire skull cavity was empty.

"Looks as though our Deity Father isn't dead," said Haldane, grimly. "He's just lost his mind."

Brogan put his hand on his partner and friend's shoulder. "Come on, Jack. Let's collect the women and get the hell out of this place."

The tinny voice of Enrico Caruso serenaded the sepia-toned darkness.

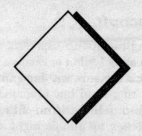

EPILOGUE

"We searched the entire underground area in and around Mrax Computers," said Podly, tapping a pencil glumly on his desk and peering up at the seated assembly. "No sign of any brain."

Patrick Brogan closed his eyes and sighed.

He opened them, and took in the welcome sight of his family, safe and sound, sitting with him on the couch to one side of Podly's desk. His arms were around Sally and Liz. Matt, as usual enjoying his visit to precinct headquarters, was busy ogling his environment. Sally leaned against Brogan, comforting him.

This was good enough for now.

He sipped at his coffee.

Good old-fashioned American java, not a

damned thing to do with espresso, cappuccino, or anything remotely Italian or Sicilian.

Off to the other side sat Jane Castle and Jack Haldane, looking tired but profoundly relieved to be through their ordeal and rid of their handcuffs.

They'd all been up all one night and half of the next, and Brogan would be very happy to get back home and under some nice warm covers. However, there were some important things to attend to first.

"We rounded up the rest of the gang, though," continued Podly. "That Carbariano included. Unfortunately, it looks as though they all had *tabula rasa* implants."

"Huh?" said Haldane.

"That would imply that their brains were wiped of both information and evidence," said Castle. "Apparently Mister Monteleone had all contingencies planned for. His crime ring has been busted, but he's slunk off to the Paris sewers, perhaps to haunt some opera."

"What about the nano-colonies?" said Haldane.

"All nanite assemblages are now just heaps of matter," said Podly. "Evidently they've self-destructed in some way. Programmed just as the others were."

"No evidence, then."

"Well, we've got the stuff from the computers. We have enough to put away Mister Monteleone for a long time. We've got enough evidence to send back to Earth and give those dummy corporations a very difficult time in court indeed." Podly made the equivalent of a Creon smile, a very rare sight indeed. "The good news, thanks to the excellent work of my *fine* police officers—and the incredible courage and intelligence of the spouse and children of my favorite lieutenant—"

Liz beamed. "Hey. That's us!"

". . . thanks to your valor and bravery, not only has an amazing criminal been defeated—if only for now—but the empire he was building has been busted. This means we have the goods on many other Demeter City underground figures we've been trying to take down for *years*!" The big, odd-shaped head nodded emphatically. "I've got a crew picking up a few of those we don't need a court order for right *now*. This, my friends, is good. *Very good!*"

Brogan shook his head doubtfully. "I don't know. If Monteleone's on the loose . . ."

Haldane raised an eyebrow. "Yeah—Whatever Monteleone *is* now. What . . . some kind of brain walking on legs?"

"What was he ever . . . a combination of human organs and nanotechnology," said Castle. "Assuming, of course, that he's still alive in any sense of the word. That waits to be seen."

"You can bet we'll be combing Mrax Computers and his other operations for information on his secrets," said Podly. "And if he shows his gray matter around here again, just maybe we'll be ready for him."

"Yeah," said Matt. "Tiny as the nanites are, they're just machines waiting for orders. I guess I proved that!" he said proudly.

"You?" said Sally.

"Okay, okay," said Matt. "Liz and me . . . " Liz glared at him. "Yeah, well, mostly Liz. I guess I've got to hand her credit for knowing a heck of a lot more about computers than I thought she did."

"Good call, Matt. Maybe you two will get along a little better now," said Brogan.

"You can bet I'm gonna start running regular checks on my new computer from now on!" said Matt.

"New computer?" said Sally.

"Yeah! For services rendered! To replace the one the nanites kinda wasted," said the teenager, pleased. "And it's gonna be turbo-charged, with a racing stripe! Metaphorically speaking, of course. Right, Podly?"

"Top of the line, m'lad," said the chief, smiling again. "We really thought it would be a good idea. . . . Government inspected, of course, with educational programs. And we're going to have your two young ones down to talk with computer experts from around the world. Along with you three. There's a lot of information about this nanotechnology and so-called 'Real Virtuality' that you're going to be able to debrief. Whatever happens, we know now that nanotechnology is capable of much more than we ever thought. This will keep scientists busy for a long, long time."

"I just hope we're ready if that gangster ever shows up again," said Haldane.

"At the very least, you can brush up on your Italian," said Castle wryly.

"You know though," said Haldane, "he kind of inspired me. Maybe I'll use all the money I'm not spending on dates to invest in a pizzeria. At least we'd get some decent pizza in Demeter City!"

"Yeah, and make sure you've got donuts, too. You bet, I'm missing those!" Brogan patted his stomach.

"That reminds me," said Podly. He hit his comm-unit. "Ms. January. I think it's time to come in here now."

"Suureeeeee," piped the broad New York accent. "Be right there, sir!"

Podly beamed. "Sir! There's a woman who knows her way around words."

Brogan leaned over toward his boss. "One thing I wanted to say, Podly. I appreciate your efforts to try and get us out of there, legal or not."

Podly nodded mordantly. "My team might have saved you a lot of grief, Brogan, if we'd been able to get in. Unfortunately, we had our *own* problems to deal with."

Podly had explained how the precinct had nearly been shut down by the nanites in the gears, so to speak. They'd been initiated late by Monteleone, though. Fortunately, as soon as Monteleone was shut down, so were the operations of his nanites. However, those tiny machines had given the precinct a good deal of trouble.

No bizarre monsters. Just shutdowns and an obvious computer takeover. However, it had been enough to distract Podly and company from rescuing their long-gone exploratory crew deep in enemy territory.

"Next time, we'll see if we can't work a little harder." Podly looked over to the Brogan family. "And you can bet that if I even knew about what was happening to you, I'd have sent out the cavalry! That nano-colony thing sealed everything up tight—but somehow managed to make everything look as though it was functioning normally."

At that moment, Betty January entered, carrying a tray. She was wearing a sedate office outfit, and her hair was tied in a bun. She wore flats, not high heels.

On the tray were cups and saucers, a pot of tea, and coffee.

Piled beside the pots were donuts.

Podly beamed. "Little Earth secret that Monteleone apparently programmed into my new Girl Friday here."

"Pul-lease, Mister Podly," said Betty. "We're in an enlightened century now. Woman January, if anything at all. And may I remind you, that I'm here to help you with the very sophisticated duties of computer systems analysis!"

Castle smiled. "Women's liberation last century. Now: android woman's liberation."

"Donuts!" said Haldane, eagerly grabbing them. "Say, Betty —what are you doing Friday night?"

"Oh! Mister Haldane," said Betty. "I was promised—no more sexual harassment on the job!"

"No harassment intended," said Haldane, munching delightedly into a honey-glazed number.

"I want to talk about hiring you away for my pizza and donut stand."

"Nothing doing," said Podly. "You brought her here, and I *like* her." He took a chocolate-covered, bite. "Hmmm. Maybe could use a few ground *amka* worms . . . but not bad. Not bad at all."

Brogan watched as his family and friends helped themselves to the treat.

Then he accepted a cup of tea himself.

There were obviously things that mankind had brought to the stars that were going to have to be dealt with in the same way they were dealt with on Earth. Like crime and war and people who threatened the well-being of all . . .

But Earth was also contributing people like these, and many more . . . People with goodwill and dreams.

And, of course, coffee, tea, and donuts.

The newest imprint of
HarperPaperbacks
presents the hottest
new writers and
the classics!

HarperPrism

THE BEST IN SCIENCE FICTION & FANTASY...

Isaac**Asimov**

C.J.**Cherryh**

UrsulaK.**LeGuin**

Robert**Gleason**

Terry**Pratchett**

Kathlyn**Starbuck**

Tad**Williams**

Gahan**Wilson**

Janny**Wurts**

The**X**-Files™

Magic: TheGathering™

..The**World**of**Darkness**™

TODAY... AND TOMORROW

PR-003